S0-AIK-795

WINNER
TAKES ALL

SHARON MAYNE

Harlequin Books

TORONTO • NEW YORK • LONDON
AMSTERDAM • PARIS • SYDNEY • HAMBURG
STOCKHOLM • ATHENS • TOKYO • MILAN
MADRID • WARSAW • BUDAPEST • AUCKLAND

To my big sister, Sue Duling
Protector and playmate in childhood,
Adviser through adolescence and
Now my closest friend

Published March 1993

ISBN 0-373-25535-7

WINNER TAKES ALL

Prologue

SHE MIGHT CALL.

Steele Erickson hoped she wouldn't, but he took the cordless telephone onto the porch with him. His son, overtired and keyed up from his sixth birthday party, had fought going to bed with the same tenacity his grandfather had displayed in the boxing ring, and Steele didn't have the energy or patience left to go another round. He didn't want the ring of the telephone to wake him.

Kevin. The thought of his son made him smile as he stretched out on a cushioned chaise lounge and set the phone on the floor beside him. Stubborn and infinitely lovable. His birth was the shining light in the darkness of his memories, like the reflection of the full moon shivering on the black waters of the lake below him.

The telephone trilled and Steele's smile twisted into a scowl. The frogs and crickets seemed to miss a note in their summer serenade, and a cloud obscured the moon. He dropped his hand to the phone, thumbed the switch to cut off the sound, but didn't speak when he brought it to his ear.

"Steele?" Her voice was soft, hesitant and helpless. He hardened his voice and his heart.

"You're too late. He's in bed."

"I couldn't call before. They wouldn't let me."

She paused, but Steele remained silent, refusing to ask who "they" were.

"I'm in trouble."

"We're divorced, Lana." Deliberately he used the stage name he'd refused to use when they were married. Her name had been Karen Stevens when they'd met in high school and Karen Erickson when they'd married the day after her graduation. Five years later, she'd won a position in a Las Vegas chorus line and changed her name to Lana Stevens. In the next two years, she'd turned into a stranger who loved the spinning of the roulette wheel more than her son or husband.

He hadn't seen her in the three years since the divorce. Nor had their son. Extravagant gifts arrived sporadically in the mail. Their timing, he knew, had more to do with fluctuations in her income than holidays or Kevin's birthday. He'd had to explain that to him again today, when neither call, card nor present had arrived.

"I'm not responsible for you or your debts anymore," he added, sure her trouble was financial.

"I . . . know." She was crying now, whimpering like a kitten taken away from its litter for the first time. "I'm so sorry."

Steele squeezed his eyes closed and willed himself to hang up, but couldn't do it. He hadn't been able to resist Karen's tears—no matter how many times she'd broken her promise to stop gambling—until she'd forged his name to drain the trust fund his father had established for Kevin. He'd called her Lana for the first time when he'd told her he was leaving and taking Kevin with him.

"Mr. Erickson," a male voice came over the line and Steele opened his eyes, "your wife owes my employer a great deal of money...."

"She's not my wife."

"She's the mother of your son."

"She gave birth to him, that's all."

The man sighed impatiently. "Be that as it may, you are her last chance to repay her debt. She seems to have exhausted every other possibility and my employer doesn't like to lose money."

"He should do more thorough credit checks."

"You, however," he continued, ignoring the interruption, "have many assets. A nice home in the Connecticut countryside, a thriving fitness center—"

"Inherited from my father *after* the divorce," Steele cut in again. "She took everything else I had in the settlement. I'm not giving her another dime." He lowered the telephone, his thumb on the switch to break the connection, but, at the man's next words, he snapped it back to his ear.

"And you have a son. Kevin, right? Six years old today."

"Are you threatening Kevin?" Steele sat bolt upright, his grip on the cordless phone tightening.

"Nothing so crass, Mr. Erickson. I'm merely suggesting he might like to spend some time with his mother."

"The court granted me full custody and she agreed. Considering the situation she's in, no judge would reverse that decision."

"We're not talking about the legal system. Just a nice visit with his mother until you come up with a hundred thou."

With a roar, Steele stood, cocked his arm and flung the phone into the yard. *The man meant to kidnap his son!* Sprinting into the house, he took the stairs three at a time and barreled into Kevin's bedroom. The night-light illuminated his small, blond head against the Snoopy-print pillow. Steele skidded to a halt, his shoulders sagging with relief. The Airedale terrier sleeping at the foot of the bed sat up and cocked her head from side to side curiously. Kevin didn't stir.

Cupping his hands over his face, Steele inhaled to calm the rage churning within him. He didn't have a hundred thousand dollars and he'd be damned if he'd sell his home or business to pay Lana's gambling debts. She'd made her bed and could damned well lie in it. But a threat against Kevin...Steele swallowed heavily, blind emotion sweeping away all rational thought.

He took another deep breath and rubbed his face as if he could wipe away his fury, then he bent and swept back the covers. "One more birthday surprise," he murmured to reassure his son as he lifted the small form into his arms.

Kevin mumbled incoherently, then nestled against Steele's chest. Dropping a kiss on the light hair so like his own, Steele hurried from the room and down the stairs, the dog at his heels.

No one, he swore, would take his son from him.

First, he'd take Kevin to safety.

Then, he'd find his ex-wife and see that the men who threatened his child went to prison . . . or hell.

1

A SOUND PIERCED Steele's heat-drugged doze, and he jerked awake, the involuntary movement forcing a pain-wracked grunt from him. He clamped his lips together and remained flat on his back, willing the adrenaline of self-preservation to pump through his veins and dispel the stupor gripping his senses.

He'd been taken by surprise this morning. He couldn't allow it to happen again.

Blinded by the bright sunlight piercing the filtered shade of the mesquite tree above him, he strained to hear beyond the ache throbbing in the muddled recesses of his head. The Colorado River flowed past his hiding place, the sound of water a taunt to his parched throat and heated flesh. A raven called, and a light breeze hummed through the branches above him. Nothing out of the or-dinary. Nothing to wake him.

How long had he been unconscious? He'd left his ho-tel room at seven-thirty and headed straight to the park-ing garage, where he'd been jumped. The sun was now high in the sky.

Great investigator he was. Stupid of him to think his search for Lana would go unnoticed, but, luckily, the thugs had been even more stupid.

His sight adjusted to the glare and he glanced to his right. The Harley he'd stolen from his assailants still leaned against the thorny branches of a desert shrub. He could see nothing to his left; that eye was swollen shut.

A movement, more sensed than seen, halted his one-eyed survey of the area. He trained his attention on the spot, tensing his protesting body, preparing it for fight or flight.

A little girl with bright blue eyes and a mass of blue-black ringlets peered around a scrawny bush. He tried to grin at her, but his split lip objected to the movement. She ducked behind her sparse screen.

On the beach a few feet beyond her, he saw a tall woman dressed in a yellow bikini top and a matching, sarong-style skirt. Her wavy, shoulder-length hair was the same color as the child's. "Jenny," she called, her voice raspy but melodic, "come look at the rock I found." She bent down.

She couldn't see him, Steele realized. The vegetation sheltering him had sprouted in a shallow depression.

Barking, a German shepherd ran to the woman's side. Now fully alert, Steele recognized the sound as the one that had awakened him. Jenny ignored her call and waddled toward him, gaining momentum with more determination than coordination. "Da-Da," she gurgled, then tumbled across his chest. Wrapping her pudgy arms around his neck, she planted a sloppy, open-mouthed kiss on his cheek.

He welcomed the coolness of her wet life vest against his chest, but a loud grunt escaped him when her small feet connected with his bruised ribs. The German shepherd barked and dashed into the grove. Growling, he loomed over Steele, his legs stiffened aggressively, ears held forward, hair raised across his shoulders and teeth bared.

Following hard on the dog's heels, the woman swooped the child off Steele's chest and retreated, clutching the girl to her breasts. The dog moved to stand in front of her, now barking at a volume that amplified the muffled drumming in Steele's head. The child's shrill protests added a clash of cymbals.

"Da-Da! Da-Da!" she cried, holding her arms out to Steele and struggling against the woman's grasp.

"That's not your daddy," the woman told her. "Hush up."

"Da-Da," the girl insisted stubbornly, although, to Steele's relief, less loudly. The woman quieted the dog too.

He swallowed with little effect. His mouth felt as dry as tissue paper. "Go," he croaked, "away."

"You're hurt," the woman said.

No joke, Sherlock, Steele thought, managing to curl his split lip into a shadow of a grin. He'd plunged, fully dressed, into the river before dragging himself to the refuge of the small grove, but he doubted the dip had improved his battered appearance.

"I'll go call an ambulance."

"No!" Pain clutched his ribs when he tried to stand. With a wary glance at the dog, he settled for shimmying his back up the tree trunk. He swallowed again, but felt like he'd only crinkled the dried tissues of his mouth. "Don't get involved."

He fixed his one-eyed gaze on the woman's face, willing her to understand. Her eyes were of such a clear, pale blue, they gave him the disconcerting feeling she could see right through him, could read his whole story and know he had no time for lolling in a hospital bed.

"Take care of your little girl," he added, thinking of Kevin safe on an isolated ranch in New Mexico with his friend, Forrest Hamilton, as bodyguard.

The blackness of her hair seemed to swim across her face. He blinked, trying to clear his vision. She glanced around the area, her expression troubled. "I can't just leave you here."

He clung to consciousness, but the dry heat sucked at his pores, luring his will into lethargy. "Have to . . . you can't help." He bit his split lip, using the pain to fight the incoming tide of oblivion. "The men . . . who did this . . . would hurt . . . a child," he added with effort, "hurt you. Go 'way."

"But you could die in this heat!"

Steele didn't argue. He slumped, unconscious, against the tree trunk.

BAILEY RICHARDS STARED at the man, easily the largest she'd ever seen. The width of his shoulders dwarfed the multi-trunked mesquite tree behind him, the bulge of his biceps stretched the short sleeves of his white knit shirt, and the breadth of his chest made his waist look impossibly narrow.

His fingers were long and blunt-shaped, his nails neatly trimmed. Apparently he'd delivered a few punches of his own—his knuckles were red and swollen. His denim-clad legs were long and his thighs, thickly powerful. His feet were in keeping with his size, his shoes big enough to hold two of Bailey's own. Athletic shoes, she noticed, studying their expensive make. The pocket of his knit shirt bore the initials of a designer line, and his blond hair was cut stylishly short.

Jenny squirmed. Bailey set her down, keeping a firm grip on her hand. The dog, Max, relaxed his guard enough to sit, but remained in position between the stranger and them, while she tried to decide what to do.

Caution told her to heed the man's advice and not get involved, but how could she just walk away and leave him? His concern for Jenny and her, despite his battered condition, touched her. From what little he'd said, she gathered he was a victim, not a criminal.

She knew there was a seamier side to the bright lights and employment opportunities the gambling town of Laughlin, Nevada provided across the Colorado River from her home in Bullhead City, Arizona. But, like other residents, she neither looked too closely nor asked questions.

She longed to call an ambulance, to let someone else take care of him. He'd seemed to think even that would involve her enough to endanger Jenny, though. Was he exaggerating? Again, she glanced around the grove, then at the barren, sandstone hills he must have crossed to reach the river from the highway. They were alone; no one was around to see what she did or didn't do.

Restless, Jenny tugged at her hand, trying to pry hers free. Swinging her back into her arms, Bailey decided there was only one way she could help the man with no one being the wiser.

She strode back to her boat, Max at her heels. Strapping Jenny into the car seat attached to the passenger chair, she explained she was going to take her to her Grandma's, then help the hurt man.

"Da-Da," Jenny cooed in apparent approval, while Bailey rummaged in the ice chest for her bottle of apple juice.

"Not Da-Da," Bailey corrected, careful to keep her emotional reaction to the term from her voice. Although Jenny was her sister's child, Bailey loved her like her own. Closing her hand around the bottle of juice, she stared sightlessly into the cooler. Bonnie had shown Jenny pictures of her blond father but, too young to understand, the child connected the term, "Da-Da," to every blond man she met.

Born eighteen months ago on the day a car accident widowed the two sisters simultaneously, Jenny would never know her father. Or her uncle or . . .

Bailey sank to her knees beside the cooler and slammed down the lid. Bending her head, she drew a deep breath and willed the paroxysm of pain to pass.

When shock had sent Bonnie into early labor, Bailey had pushed her own grief aside to find the strength to hold her sister's hand while she gave birth on that day of death. And Bonnie's subsequent willingness to share the gift of life still helped her face each new day.

"Stop it." The sound of her own voice startled her and she raised her head. She'd gone through all the stages of grief, anger at the world, at her husband, at herself and all the what ifs.

Now only the ache of loss remained, an ache that waxed when she was idle and waned when she kept busy. Inhaling deeply, she gave Jenny the bottle of juice, then checked the straps on her niece's life vest and steered the boat upriver.

TWENTY MINUTES LATER, Bailey returned to the beach where she'd found the battered stranger. As she'd expected, her mother had been only too happy to care for her only grandchild until Bonnie got off work.

Pulling the boat onto the shore, she told Max to stay, took a plastic jug of water from the cooler and grabbed a bucket. Filling it with river water, she returned to the grove. The man still slumped against the tree. Setting down the jug, she gently poured the bucket of water over him from head to toe. He came to, sputtering.

"I'm going to help you," she told him, kneeling by his side, "but you have to help me."

"Go away."

"Drink this." She twisted off the top of the water jug and handed it to him. His one good eye glared at her, but he took the container and drank thirstily. "It's over a hundred degrees and not quite noon," she said. "It's going to get hotter and lying on the ground is the worse thing you can do. If you're not already dehydrated, you will be. The desert in July is not a friendly place."

"Leave me water." He returned the emptied jug. "I'll stay here until dark, then go."

"You're going now." Bailey set the jug aside.

"Thought you wanted to save me, not kill me."

"I have a boat and can take you to a safe place. No one need know."

His good eye widened. "Why?"

Images floated through Bailey's mind, while she struggled to answer his simple question. Another man's battered face. A mangled truck. A . . .

She dropped a mental curtain over the vivid memories. "How do you start your bike? We need it to get you to the boat."

"Key's in the ignition. Gas is on the right handle, clutch on the left." He pushed away from the tree trunk to stand, but swayed instead, clenching his jaw in pain and wrapping his arms around his ribs. Bailey grabbed his shoulder. Her fingers barely stretched across its width.

"Is anything broken?" she asked.

"Just bruised. Is the boat far?"

She shook her head.

"Start the bike. I'll get up in a minute."

"Sit still." Bailey stood and unknotted the light cotton fabric wrapped sarong-style at her waist. She saw his head tilt, his gaze traveling up her bare legs to her bikini-clad torso.

"Nice," he murmured. "Always was a sucker for long legs."

Bailey blinked in surprise. The last thing she'd expected from him was flirtation, and she didn't welcome its reminder of the difference in their sexes. All she wanted to do was help him as one human being to another.

She knelt by his side, ending his appreciative survey. "You must not be too badly hurt, if you can still leer," she said, frowning and gesturing toward his rib cage with the rectangle of yellow material. He obediently lifted his arms from his sides, but winced and gave up the attempt to raise them higher.

"Long as I've got one good eye, I can recognize a beautiful woman." He looked at her over his shoulder, the undamaged side of his mouth lifting in a grin.

A deep, turquoise blue eye, she noticed, unable to halt the thought that he, too, would be quite attractive when his face healed.

With one end of the makeshift skirt in each hand, she stretched her arms around him, trying to cross the fabric on his opposite side. When her breasts brushed against him, she jerked backwards, flustered by a jolt of sensual awareness at the intimate contact.

"How many men did it take to deck you?" she asked to cover her discomfiture. Handing him one end of the material, she walked around him to wrap its length around his broad rib cage.

"Three. Two to hold me and one to do the beating."

She took both ends of the fabric, knelt and, angry at her body's unwanted reaction to him, knotted them with too much force.

He gasped.

"Too tight?" she asked, instantly contrite.

He took an experimental breath, then shook his head.

"I'll help you up."

He looked at her dubiously.

Bailey stood. "I'm five foot eight and weigh a hundred and thirty pounds. I won't break."

"I'm six-four and top you by ninety pounds. You can't lift me."

She bent to grasp his arm. "Not lift, help."

"You're one stubborn lady."

Bailey grinned and tugged at the rock-hard bicep in her hands. "Wait until you get to know my *bad* traits."

While he struggled to his feet, she slipped beneath his arm and slid hers around his waist, careful not to touch his ribs. A groan escaped his lips, and sweat broke out on his forehead, but he stood slowly.

Suddenly his face paled; he swayed and clutched her to him. Wrapping both arms around his waist, Bailey supported him with her body from head to foot, agonizingly aware of the hard contours of his masculine frame, the thud of his laboring heart and the heat of him emanating through his clothes and onto her skin, bare save for the tiny strips of her bikini.

As soon as she thought he could stand alone, she stepped away. "Lean against the tree while I start the bike," she ordered. He obeyed, watching and directing while she experimentally ran through the gears. Then he sidled around the tree, straddled the bike and reached around her to grip the middle of the handlebars, leaving the controls to her.

His broad chest pressed against her back, his thighs cradled her hips, and his arms rested against the sides of her breasts. "Maybe you'd be better off walking," Bailey suggested in a strangled voice she barely recognized as her own.

"Just holding my head up makes me dizzy." His breath caressed her ear as he rested his chin on her shoulder. "Try not to hit any bumps."

"Hold on." Telling herself her reactions were normal for a woman in such intimate contact with a stranger, Bailey moved the bike forward. While she cautiously navigated around bushes and rocks, she told him her name and asked his.

"Steele, with an e, Erickson," he answered.

"Steele?" she echoed disbelievingly.

"Father was a boxer." His voice was weak, and his head weighed more heavily on her shoulder. She risked a glance at him; his face was gray.

An odd name, she thought, but fitting, and his condition made a lie unlikely.

Despite a few unavoidable bumps that wrung groans from Steele, they reached the boat without mishap. Max barked a greeting, but remained in the boat at Bailey's command. Steele mumbled, "Hot," stumbled off the bike and into the water, where he fell face forward. Bailey rushed after him.

"I'm okay," he muttered, when she sat him up, "but the water's too cold." He shivered and tried to struggle to his feet.

"Because you're overheated. Stay in." She crouched beside him, ready to catch his head if his chin started to sink. He sighed and closed his eyes.

Filling her free hand with water, Bailey ran her fingers through his hair and over his forehead to cool him further. He didn't open his eyes. Staring into his face, she didn't fight the tender feelings stirring deep within her. His huge size made him seem all the more vulnerable. She slipped her arms around him, allowing him to rest his head on her shoulder and his back against her breasts.

She was only remotely aware of murmuring soft reassurances as she pressed her cheek to his temple. She held him until her own body grew chilled. "Can you help me get your bike in the boat?"

"Wipe off the handles and leave it here." His good eye fluttered open. "It's theirs. Maybe they'll think I drowned."

He lurched to his feet, hauled himself over the side of the boat and collapsed, his strength clearly exhausted. Bailey hurriedly wiped their fingerprints off the bike, then climbed into the boat and roared upriver.

When she neared her home, though, she abruptly let up on the throttle.

A familiar figure waited on the small pier. Max barked a happy greeting, but Bailey grimaced and glanced back at Steele sprawled on the floor in the back of the boat.

Short of tossing him overboard, there was no way to hide him. She should've known her sister would show up. Sighing, she masked her dismay with a big smile and maneuvered the boat toward the dock.

2

"I KNEW SOMETHING was up, just knew it! Where's Jenny?" Bonnie yelled over the rumble of the idling boat engine, her attention torn between the empty baby seat beside Bailey and the man lying prone in the back of the boat.

"At Mom and Dad's." Bailey cut the engine. Bonnie tossed her a rope and scurried down the ladder into the boat.

"I was at the registration desk, handing a gray-haired couple their room key," she explained, "when I got an upsetting mental flash of you in your boat, so I took my lunch hour and rushed right over." Max shoved his nose beneath her hand. Petting him absently, she bent to peer down at the unconscious stranger, then drew back, appalled at his battered appearance. "I *knew* you were up to no good! I didn't think it had anything to do with Jenny, but—"

"You had to stick your nose in my business," Bailey interrupted with a grin Bonnie knew only too well.

Bailey had used it on her since they were kids. It always meant her sister had gotten herself in trouble and needed help. "Don't even start," Bonnie warned, shaking her head and starting up the ladder. "I changed my mind, I don't want to know."

"You said I should take an interest in men again," Bailey said, her tone suspiciously mild.

Bonnie spun around to face her. "I didn't mean you should haul beat-up strangers home!"

"How could I leave a fantastic body like this lying on the beach? His name is Steele Erickson. I thought you'd approve."

"That body needs a doctor."

"He needs out of this sun. Help me get him to the house." Bailey wet a rag and knelt to bathe the stranger's face. "Time to wake up," she cooed. "A nice, cool, comfortable bed is waiting."

"You do mean a hospital bed," Bonnie said, realizing she had to try to keep her foolhardy sister out of trouble. She didn't for a minute believe the guy was who he said he was.

"No hospital," he objected, opening his good eye and looking straight at Bonnie. He grunted with surprise and glanced at Bailey. Blinking rapidly, he sucked in his breath and again looked at Bonnie, an expression of horror forming on his face.

"No, you're not seeing double," Bailey assured him hurriedly. "We're identical twins. This is my sister, Bonnie Hayword." His sigh of relief was audible. "She took twenty minutes to follow me out the birth canal and cautious has been her middle name ever since."

"We don't need to get him to the house." Bonnie ignored the introduction. "The ambulance personnel can bring a stretcher. I'll go call."

"Don't you dare!" Bailey jumped to her feet and pulled her away from the ladder.

Bonnie glared at her. "Bailey, this isn't—"

"Some stray animal? I know that! He's a human being, and he's hurt. Don't you think—"

"He deserves help? Of course, but he can get that in a hospital instead of your house! And don't call me a—"

"Chicken?" Bailey grinned.

"That taunt worked on me when we were kids, and you were up to no good. I'm talking common sense now, Bails. You're twenty-eight years old. The man is beat up, he's got trouble written all over him, and whoever did this—"

"May come after me. Exactly. If I call an ambulance, they'll know I found him. I had no choice but to bring him here. He said they'd even hurt—"

"Jenny?" Bonnie finished. "Who'd hurt Jenny?" Turning in unison with her sister, Bonnie looked at the man, who stared back at them, glassy-eyed.

"Do you always finish one another's sentences?" he mumbled.

Bonnie glanced at her sister, shrugged, nodded and returned her attention to Steele, silently demanding an answer to her question.

"Same people who threatened to kidnap my son." He spoke more clearly, but watching his throat work when he swallowed, Bonnie could see the effort it cost him. "Ex-wife's a gambler. Compulsive." He scowled. "They want me to pay her debts or they'll snatch Kevin. Trying to find her so she can lead me to them, and I can call in the cops. Got jumped." He closed his good eye.

Soft touch that she was, Bailey gasped, but Bonnie saw no reason to believe him. "Where's your son?"

"Safe place. With a friend." His voice was a thread of sound.

"Let's get him to bed." Bailey knelt by his side and slipped an arm beneath his shoulders. Bonnie reluctantly followed suit. The guy was hurt, she had to admit, and lying in the sun while she argued with her stubborn twin wouldn't help him.

His face drained of color when they got him on his feet, but he reached for the ladder to the dock on his own.

"Bonnie, you go first," Bailey ordered.

Reaching the pier, Bonnie looked down. The man had propped one foot on a middle rung, but seemed unable to slide his hands higher up the ladder supports to haul himself up. Bailey stood behind him, fluttering her hands uselessly.

"What's the matter, Bails?" she asked with feigned innocence. "Just put your hands on those great buns and push!"

Bailey whipped her hands behind her back. "Want to change places?" she asked.

"No way. I don't bring strange men home and fondle their buns."

"Go ahead." The guy looked over his shoulder at Bailey. "Fondle. It's the only way I'm going to get up this ladder."

"On the count of three?" Bailey swallowed nervously and gingerly planted her hands on the muscled mounds in front of her.

He counted, Bailey shoved, and Bonnie caught him under his arms. His weight forced her to stagger backward, then sink to the ground. Bailey tried to catch him from behind, but tripped and fell, too. Max leapt from the boat to join the fun and lick their faces.

Bonnie heard the man groan when she extricated herself from under him. "He could have internal injuries," she worried.

"No," he mumbled, "not that kind of pain. Ribs hurt, head hurts, but . . . mainly hot, weak."

"How do you know?" she asked, still skeptical of him.

"Run fitness center. Know anatomy."

"Where?"

"Connecticut."

Bailey cut her off before she could ask another question. "Let's get him into the house. We can hear the details later."

With their arms around his waist and his arms over their shoulders, they passed through the gate of the fence separating the dock from the yard and followed Max uphill.

"Your bed?" Bonnie objected when they entered the house and Bailey headed for her room.

"It's queen-size. He's too big for the bunk beds in . . ." she paused " . . . the other bedroom."

As soon as they got him to the bed, the man immediately lapsed into unconsciousness. Apparently accepting him as one of his charges, Max lay down at the foot of the bed. Bailey turned the air-conditioning on high.

Bonnie took a framed photograph from the nightstand and stored it in a drawer. "We need the room," she said firmly, staring down Bailey's frown. Her sister clung to such mementos of her marriage to an unhealthy degree, in her opinion. "Shouldn't you get some soap and water to clean him up?"

Bailey used scissors to snip through his shirt and the yellow skirt she'd used to bind his ribs. When she parted the fabric, Bonnie gasped at the livid bruises on his chest, ribs and stomach.

"You should've left him on the beach and called the police or a hospital anonymously," she said, renewing their argument, but bending over her side of the bed to help tug at his jeans. "Bringing a complete stranger home is bad enough, but one in this condition . . ."

Her lecture fell on deaf ears, she suspected, watching Bailey wet a washcloth and dab at the man's battered face, then bathe his arms and chest. A smattering of reddish-blond hair darkened as it grew moist, emphasizing the deep cleft between his hard, round pectoral muscles.

Bailey skimmed the cloth downward, and the man's flat stomach rippled in reflex. She skipped over the black low-cut briefs then sponged his massive thighs. He did have a fantastic build, Bonnie admitted silently.

"He must be a bodybuilder or professional athlete," Bailey commented. "Bodies like this are made, not born."

"He could be anything," Bonnie retorted. "Doctor, lawyer, thief, rapist, murderer . . ."

"Only a good man would worry about a child's safety in his condition."

Steele woke when they sat him up to bind his ribs with an elastic athletic bandage, then eagerly accepted the aspirin Bailey offered.

"What is it with you, Bails?" The soft concern she saw in her sister's eyes worried Bonnie. "You haven't looked at a man in a year and a half, and now you're fussing over a complete stranger!"

"Are you hungry?" Bailey ignored her and addressed her patient. His stomach growled as if responding to the mention of food.

"I'll be right back," Bailey promised. Bonnie trailed behind her as she left the room, again trying to persuade her to call an ambulance.

STEELE CLOSED his eyes and hoped Bailey would continue to resist her sister's urgings to get him to a hospital.

He didn't need a doctor; he needed rest. His head still ached, and the smallest movement set his body throbbing. He wanted to sleep, but he hadn't eaten since the previous evening and hoped food would restore his strength. To keep himself awake, he looked around the room.

A large window opposite his bed framed a view of a green lawn. Dotted with shade trees and colorful flowerbeds, it led down to the river. A child's swing set and sandbox stood in front of the fenced-off boat dock. Jagged, stone-faced mountains rose skyward on the other side of the river. The room itself was furnished with white wicker furniture on mint green carpeting. The print pattern of the bedspread, drapes and chair pillows added accents of peach to the color scheme. Antique perfume bottles decorated a vanity. The room was feminine without being frilly. He saw no sign of a male occupant and remembered Bonnie's comment that Bailey hadn't looked at a man in over a year. Why?

Too bad he couldn't stay long enough to find out. She had great legs and, despite his pain, he'd been very aware of each contact with her soft, feminine curves while she'd helped him on the beach. He wouldn't repay her kindness by involving her in his troubles, though.

Bailey bustled back into the bedroom, carrying a tray table, which she set across his lap. She'd covered her bikini with a short terry-cloth beach robe. About to confess his disappointment, he saw her twin appear behind her and thought better of it.

Bonnie's hostile behavior stemmed from concern for her sister, he figured, and she wouldn't find a suggestive comment, however complimentary, reassuring.

"It isn't much," Bailey said, pulling a wicker rocking chair to the side of the bed. "If this stays down, I'll fix you something more solid later."

Steele looked at the tray. Rice floated in a clear broth in a china bowl. Saltines lay on a matching plate next to it. No, it didn't look like much, but it smelled heavenly.

Chicken-based, the broth possessed a rich flavor he was sure hadn't come from a can. Not only was Bailey gorgeous and kind, she could cook, too. "This is wonderful," he told her honestly. She smiled her pleasure at his praise.

Bonnie only gave him a few minutes to enjoy the soup before she claimed the chair on the opposite side of the bed and resumed her interrogation. "Just how much trouble are you in?"

"I'm not sure," Steele admitted. "The last address I had for Lana was in Laughlin, but no one's seen her for two weeks. I've been asking a lot of questions, which must be why three men jumped me in a parking garage early this morning and told me to pay up and shut up."

"Why don't you go to the police?"

"They can't do much unless Kevin was kidnapped and I'm not waiting for that to happen."

The two sisters exchanged a long look, but remained silent while Steele finished his meal. "I appreciate what you've done for me," he said when he'd all but licked the bowl clean. "The less you know, though, the better. I'll rest for a few hours, then get out of here."

Bonnie looked relieved; Bailey shook her head. "The only place you can go from here is a hospital."

"And have them ask a lot of questions? Draw attention to myself?" Steele was firm. "No way."

"You should have X rays, at the very least." Bailey reached to take his tray, but he caught her hand.

"I'm not seriously hurt, believe me. You've fed me, wrapped my ribs. All I need is rest."

"We'll see."

"Bailey!" Bonnie protested. "Do what he says!"

"We'll see," Bailey repeated and drew her hand from Steele's. She took his tray and handed it to her sister. Before he could argue further, she pulled all but one of the pillows from behind his back, splayed her fingers against his chest and pushed him into a prone position. Then she placed an ice pack over his blackened eye and spread a soothing salve over his tender lips. "Sleep," she commanded, then turned to Bonnie. "Hadn't you better get back to work?"

Deciding he needed his strength to combat the forceful Bailey, Steele remained silent, but watched the women leave, his one-eyed gaze automatically dropping to their legs. Bonnie's simple sundress extended to her knees, while Bailey's robe hit her at mid-thigh. Identical twins or not, he thought Bailey had the better set of legs, although he had to admit he'd be hard-pressed to explain why.

He wasn't exactly an impartial judge, he realized, when Bailey turned at the door and smiled at him. "Sleep well," she said, then called Max and ushered the dog from the room before she closed the door. Wishing he could wake up with her beside him and in condition to take full advantage of such a situation, Steele drifted off to sleep.

BONNIE'S SILENCE was louder than words when Bailey joined her in the kitchen. She'd already heard her slam the tray table on the counter. Now she jerked open drawers, cabinets and the refrigerator, then banged them closed. Careful to stay out of her way, Bailey put Steele's dishes in the dishwasher. Bonnie poured a glass of milk, helped herself to the rest of the broth and sat down at the table in the windowed breakfast nook facing the backyard.

"Put yourself in his place," Bailey said, sliding onto the opposite bench. "What if someone were threatening Jenny?"

"I'd go to the police."

"And if they couldn't do anything?"

Bonnie had picked up her spoon, but she returned it to the bowl without tasting the broth. "Don't get involved in this, Bails, please," she pleaded. Her angry expression crumpled. "I couldn't bear to lose you, too."

Bailey reached across the table and patted her hand. "Nothing's going to happen to me."

Bonnie smiled wanly and returned her attention to her lunch. After a few minutes, she asked, "You're going to help him find his wife, aren't you?" She pushed her bowl away, although she'd only taken a few swallows.

"Ex-wife," Bailey corrected, vaguely realizing she felt possessive of Steele, then quickly dismissing the thought. "I just want to help him get better."

"Why?" Bonnie slammed her hand against the table in frustration. "You haven't taken an interest in anything outside our family since the accident. Why now? Why this?"

Unable to endure the pain she saw on her sister's face, Bailey turned toward the window and stared at the playset in front of the fenced-off dock. Although it was empty, she pictured a small figure sailing high in one of the swings.

"He's gone," Bonnie said flatly.

Bailey swung her gaze back to her sister, not surprised at her perception. She was used to it.

"Helping this guy isn't going to change that," Bonnie added more gently.

"The guy has a name, Steele Erickson. You wouldn't be so eager for me to kick him out, if you'd let yourself see him as a person. As a father protecting his son."

Bonnie nodded reluctantly, acknowledging her point. "You didn't know he was a father when you brought him home, though. Whatever possessed you?"

"His first concern was for Jenny and me. How could I just leave him?" Bailey didn't wait for an answer. "And then," she added, forcing herself to confront her feelings honestly, "when I touched him, something came alive inside of me." She lowered her gaze, then raised it with effort. "I remembered I was a woman, with a woman's needs. It was like I'd been sleepwalking and—"

"And you woke up when you found a bruised and battered man on the beach?" Bonnie's voice and face were incredulous.

"Can you imagine what he looks like without a black eye and split lip? Two of those gorgeous blue eyes with that naturally blond hair?"

Bonnie stared at her for a moment, then smiled slyly. "I don't know about you, honey, but when you gave him his sponge bath, his face was the last thing I was looking at!"

Bailey laughed. "I thought you were too busy reading me the riot act to notice!"

"Oh, I noticed, all right." Bonnie drank her milk, then turned serious. "What I don't understand is why, after all this time, you get the hots for a beat-up stranger."

"He was at my mercy?" Bailey suggested with a grin, but her sister's expression remained somber.

Bonnie set down her glass and folded her arms on the table. "I can understand you brought him home out of a Good Samaritan impulse, and lust for his body, but those aren't good enough reasons to get involved with thugs threatening to kidnap a child."

"I didn't say—"

"You don't have to say it! I can read you like an open book! Why are you going to help him? What aren't you telling me?"

Bailey jumped from the table as if distance could provide a mental barrier between them. "Want more milk?" she asked, opening the refrigerator and hiding her face behind the door.

"What aren't you telling me?"

Sighing, Bailey grabbed a soda and returned to the table. She'd tried to ignore the suspicions stirring in her mind over the past few months, but Steele's story reinforced them. Something fishy was definitely going on in Laughlin.

"Have you ever thought it odd how the Sunburst," she named the casino that employed the two of them, "promoted you to head of reservations and me to manager of the beauty salon within six months after the accident?"

Bonnie shook her head. "We're both good at our jobs and I know I worked even harder, just to keep myself busy."

"Why did your former boss leave?"

"She got a better offer in the Vegas casino."

"So did mine."

Bonnie's eyes widened. "You think they were given jobs in Vegas to make room for us?"

Bailey nodded.

"Why?"

"Think about it." Bailey kept her mind a blank, not wanting her sister to read her conclusions. She popped open the can of cola and drank from it while she waited.

"They felt sorry for us?"

"That's what I thought when I got a raise shortly after I came back to work, but what better way to keep us around?"

Bonnie shook her head. "Why bother? Hairdressers and registration clerks aren't hard to replace."

"To watch us." Bailey didn't give her sister a chance to ask why. "As soon as I came back, I started getting more local customers, some of the higher-ups' wives." She rolled her eyes. "And mistresses. After giving me their condolences, they started asking a lot of questions about the accident."

Bonnie furrowed her brow. "That's natural, isn't it? No one, not the police or even the insurance company, figured out why the truck went off the road."

"Driver error," Bailey reminded her. She stood and paced in front of the breakfast nook. "But you and I both know what a careful driver Cliff was." She fell silent for a moment. "My new clients seemed more interested in what *I* thought. I told them it didn't much matter how it happened. It was all I could do to accept that it had." She paused and drew a deep breath, the pain the memory evoked never far away. "I didn't think much of it at the time other than to wonder if they were ghouls getting a kick out of my misery. I finally started saying I didn't want to talk about it, and most of them stopped asking for me."

"Maybe they were like people who chase fire trucks and ambulances," Bonnie suggested, "fascinated by the tragedy."

"I don't think so."

"What else could it be?"

Bailey sat back down. "I think they wanted to know if I suspected anything."

"Suspected what?" Bonnie's face reflected a dawning, but unwilling, comprehension.

"That there wasn't any accident. That the truck was forced off the road. That Cliff and Ron and..." Bailey drew a deep, steadying breath "...were murdered."

3

"WHY?"

Bonnie's question hung in the air long after she'd left for work. Bailey didn't have an answer for it. She had a strong suspicion, but Bonnie had refused to even consider the idea. And that hurt. Without her twin's support, Bailey felt bereft.

To keep busy, she mixed a hearty beef stew in her Crock-Pot, then wandered outside. Bending over the daylilies bordering the front of her stucco bungalow, she pinched off spent blossoms and pulled intruding weeds. The mindless exercise usually soothed the rough edges of her blue moods, but by the time she'd worked through the flowerbeds around the house to the backyard, she felt no better.

Hollyhocks stood in front of the posts supporting the redwood deck, and morning glories climbed the lattice between them. She alternately sang and hummed while she groomed the flowers, but the melody reflected her melancholy.

"Are you sure you've accepted they're gone?" Bonnie had asked. "Sure you're not dwelling on the past and looking for revenge? An explanation for the unexplainable?"

"If there's a chance someone deliberately ran Cliff's truck off the road," Bailey had countered, "wouldn't you

want to know? Wouldn't you want those responsible
punished?"

By responding to Bonnie's question with a question,
she'd avoided answering it, but now it haunted her. In
recent months, Bonnie had not only started dating again,
she'd sold the home she'd shared with Ron. They had to
break with the past and go forward with their lives, she'd
told Bailey. For the first time, her twin had taken the lead
and had urged her to move on, too. But Bailey couldn't
bear to part with the riverfront property she'd land-
scaped herself or the house that had held so many dreams
and still held happy memories.

Was she chasing ghosts? Living in the past? Did her
suspicions have a basis in fact, or had they risen from the
holes the accident had left in her life?

How could she go forward with her life until she knew?

She'd lost more than Bonnie had, which was why she
needed to pursue any possibility of a connection between their husbands' deaths and Steele's ex-wife's disappearance.

Better not to involve her sister, though. Bonnie still
had Jenny. She didn't fear risking her own empty life, but
she couldn't endanger theirs. It was bad enough that Ron
had been riding in Cliff's truck. Not to mention . . .

Refusing to finish the thought, Bailey mounted the
steps of the deck and sat down on the cushioned glider.
Max left the shade of the flowering mimosa tree in the
yard and joined her, settling at her feet. "What should I
do?" she asked him. If anything happened to her, her
parents and sister would suffer, but how could she pass
up the chance to explore her suspicions by helping Steele
find his ex-wife? Max sat up and rested his head on her

knee. Petting him, she found a measure of solace to clear her mind.

She had no choice. By helping Steele, she'd help herself.

Staring at the sun sinking toward the sanctuary of the mountains across the river, she surrendered to the sadness that stalked her. Giving voice to it, she crooned a ballad of lost love and the bittersweet pain of living.

"A BESSIE SMITH TUNE?" Steele had waited until the song ended before he pushed through the kitchen door.

Startled, Bailey jerked her head toward him. The German shepherd growled and raised his head, then, apparently remembering Steele was no threat, lay down and closed his eyes.

"Robert Johnson," she answered with a wan smile, naming another classic blues singer of the thirties. "Did I wake you?" She stood as he crossed the deck to the glider seat. "How do you feel?" She pressed a hand to his forehead.

"Much better. Stiff, but not so weak and woozy." Steele stared into the shadows darkening her light eyes, shadows that echoed the anguish he'd heard in her voice. He'd been listening at the door, hesitating to intrude on her privacy, yet unable to turn away. Her palm felt soft and cool against his forehead, but he wanted to reverse their positions and offer her comfort. "How about you?" He grasped her hand and, careful not to disturb the dog, took a seat on the glider, drawing her down next to him. "It sounds like you're not just singing the blues. Want to talk?"

She didn't pull her hand from his, but she remained silent, studying him with her otherworldly, light blue eyes.

"Or would it help if I just held you?" he suggested. When she still didn't answer, he gently slid his arm around her and guided her head to his shoulder. "Touch is a wonderful thing," he said, ignoring the fact that she felt as rigid as a broomstick in his light embrace. "It says so much more than words, if only we'd trust it." He talked on, soothing her with his voice, knowing the tone was more important than the sense of his words.

Slowly she relaxed, raising her legs onto the glider and tucking them beneath her, then curling her body farther into his embrace. Gradually he stopped talking, but continued the rhythmic swaying of the glider. Resting his cheek on the top of her head, he stroked her arm with his fingertips. Touch worked both ways, he realized. The feel of her smooth skin and silky hair soothed the frayed fringes within his own mind.

After long moments, she raised her head and sat back. "Thank you," she said softly. "I needed that. I was feeling very alone."

"You're welcome." With their faces close together, their gazes caught and held. Steele felt a fragile bond form between them, transcending their status as strangers.

"The swelling is down," she murmured and lifted her hand to his face—an excuse to touch him, he hoped. Her fingertips skimmed lightly over his blackened eye and down his cheek, then lingered on his split lip. Steele blew a light kiss on them as she withdrew her hand.

"You're an excellent nurse. How can I ever thank you?"

The shadows crept back into her eyes. She looked away from him, then rose and crossed to the railing.

Steele followed her gaze across the green oasis of the yard to the river and beyond, to the mountains on the opposite shore, dark against a sky streaked with the crimson and gold of the setting sun.

"There is something you can do," she said, her voice so soft he had to strain to hear her. "If you're sure you feel up to talking." She turned back to him, her eyes bright with determination.

"I'm not up to running any marathons, but my head's clear enough for me to listen."

"Do you have a picture of your ex-wife?"

Steele frowned at the unexpected question. "Why?"

"I'm a hairdresser in Laughlin. I may have seen her."

Although surprised by her request, Steele stood and went into the house to fetch his wallet. He'd pretty much hit a dead end in his search. If Bailey could come up with a new lead, he wasn't going to turn it down. He couldn't figure out how a picture of Lana could help her, though.

He found his jeans on the floor by the bed and pulled his wallet from the back pocket. For a moment, he considered donning the long pants, but the air outside was still warm, despite the sinking sun and the shade cast by the louvered trellis roofing the deck. His briefs were cotton, not transparent nylon, and, he decided, no more revealing than European-style swim trunks.

When he returned to the deck, he found Bailey comfortably ensconced on top of the flat railing, her back against a post, one long, lovely leg bent and the other stretched out beside it. She must have caught his admiring glance because she shot him a bold one of her own.

"Should I have put on my jeans?" he asked, aware she'd traded her yellow bikini for light blue cotton shorts and a white, sleeveless blouse embroidered with pastel flowers.

"Not on my account." She smiled, a frank woman-to-man smile. "I have to admit I've only seen bodies like yours on television or in movies."

He grinned and handed her the photograph. "The exhibitionist in my bodybuilding past still loves an appreciative audience. I'd flex for you, but I don't think my ribs could bear it."

"I'll take a rain check," she responded solemnly.

Steele hadn't expected her to take his offer seriously and felt an unfamiliar heat rise in his cheeks. Turning away from her quickly, he took a seat on the glider. Although he was accustomed to exhibiting himself onstage, the thought of a private performance in front of this woman flustered him. Unless, of course, she wanted to touch as well as look... He shifted in his seat as a more familiar heat stirred lower in his body.

Bailey raised her gaze from the picture. "She's very beautiful and looks vaguely familiar," she said, "but I'm sure I've never done her hair. What's her name?"

"Lana—" Steele didn't hide his distaste for the name or the woman who bore it "—Stevens. She was doing a solo song and dance act at the Colorado Belle recently. You might have seen a publicity poster. She quit two weeks ago without notice. Told her boss she had a better offer, but he doesn't know where. None of the other casinos hired her. I checked."

"I could take this to work." She waved the photograph she held. Steele immediately shook his head, but she plowed on. "And see if any of the other women know her."

"After what happened to me? I couldn't let you do it." He stood and extended his hand for the picture. She whipped it behind her back. He reached around her and gripped her wrist.

Resisting his gentle but firm pressure, she stared up at him mutinously. "I want to do this."

"No." Steele bent and pressed a light kiss on her lips. He'd meant only to demonstrate his gratitude for what she'd already done and what she now offered. But at the first, sweet contact with her yielding mouth, the desire for her simmering in the recesses of his consciousness leapt to the fore, hot and strong.

He sprang back, knowing if he didn't, not even the tenderness of his split lip or bruised ribs would prevent him from pulling her close and deepening the kiss.

"I'm sorry." He didn't know if he was apologizing for kissing her or for refusing her help, but she didn't question him.

"I want to do this for myself, not you," she insisted.

"Why?" Steele moved back to the safe distance of the glider, yielding her the photograph of Lana. For now.

"You said she was a gambler, right?"

Steele nodded.

"And she owes someone a lot of money. Any idea who?"

He shook his head. "I guess I expected to walk up to her door and ask her, but her neighbors haven't seen her lately. Her landlord said her rent's overdue." He sighed. "About all I can do is wait until my face heals and file a missing person's report with the police."

"I thought you didn't want to involve the police."

"I don't know what else I can do. I can prove no one's seen Lana. If they have better luck finding her, she'll lead me to the men threatening Kevin."

"Why wait until your face heals? Don't you want the police to arrest the guys who beat you?"

"Oh, I want them punished, all right." Steele glowered at the memory. "But they were just hired thugs obeying orders. I want to follow them to their boss, and I can't do that if they're in jail for assault and battery."

"You got a good look at them?"

"One of them. I'm pretty sure I've seen him before."

"At the Sunburst Casino?"

Stunned, Steele blurted out, "How did you know?"

"That's where I work, where my husband worked, and I think there's something rotten going on." She eyed him, obviously pleased with the accuracy of her guess. "Which is why I want to help you find your ex-wife."

"Your husband?" Steele kept his voice bland, but he felt a distinct stab of disappointment.

She nodded and pulled her knees up to her chest. Wrapping her fingers around her ankles, she lowered her head to her knees. "He died," she said, her voice muffled, "eighteen months ago."

"I'm sorry." For her pain, he silently added. He couldn't pretend to be sorry she was now single.

She raised her head. "The police decided it was an accident. His truck went off the side of a mountain. Bonnie's husband was with him. He died, too." She stared straight ahead of her. "But I'm beginning to think he was run off the road."

"Why?"

"Cliff was a blackjack dealer at the Sunburst. One of the pit bosses asked him if he'd like to work a private party. Very exclusive with high stakes. All very hush-hush." She paused, seemingly lost in her memories. "Tips at those affairs can be fantastic, so he didn't think twice about it. Laughlin doesn't get as many high rollers as Vegas. It's pretty much a middle-class gambling town, a lot of retirees dressed in Bermuda shorts."

She looked at Steele, then, as if to help focus her thoughts. "Anyway, it was a two-day affair with long shifts. Hal, the pit boss, promised him an extra three days off from the casino when he got back. Ron was a fireman and had time coming, so they planned to go on a fishing and camping trip."

She started talking faster, no longer seeing him, Steele suspected. "Cliff wasn't due home from the job until the morning of the third day, but he didn't stay over the second night. All he told me was that he'd flown in a helicopter to a ritzy place in the Dead Mountains, but the party was lousy. He didn't want to talk about it, which wasn't like him. He gave me his money and called Ron to see if he could leave early. Ron said yes, Cliff loaded the truck, kissed me and left."

When she fell silent again, Steele prodded her gently. "What makes you think his truck was run off the road?"

"He was upset about something, I'm sure of it. He even tried to break his promise to take—" She broke off, blinking rapidly, then resumed without finishing what she'd started to say. "There's no club registered in the Dead Mountains, I've checked, which means there's no legal supervision. I think Cliff figured out the games were fixed and insisted on leaving. He took a lot of pride in his job and loved the combination of skill and chance in blackjack. He hated cheating in any form."

She went on to explain how both Bonnie and she had been promoted at the Sunburst and how her new clients had asked a lot of questions about the accident. But Steele's attention focused on her description of the party. Lana, he knew, would've jumped at a chance to entertain at such an affair. Once there, she would've wormed her way onto the gambling tables, where she could've lost heavily, then not been allowed to leave when she couldn't cover her losses.

He still wasn't willing to allow Bailey to flash Lana's picture around her beauty salon, though, and he told her so. He would, however, pretend Lana had mentioned a party in the mountains when he reported her disappearance to the police.

"But they won't know where it is anymore than I do," Bailey protested, "and as soon as they start searching, you can bet all trace of gambling will disappear from the place. And there'll be no sign of Lana, either." She jumped down from her perch on the railing and joined him on the glider seat. "We need to get an invitation to one of those parties." She sat sideways, one arm on the back of the glider, leaning toward him intensely. "Check into the Sunburst and throw around big bills. Act like fools begging to be parted from our money. Word will get around. Then—" she gave him no chance to interrupt "— once we're inside the private casino, I know how to watch for cheating. Cliff told me, and my dad was a dealer, too. You could keep an eye out for Lana. We'll lose money, then beg for a chance to come back and recoup our losses. When we're invited back, we'll notify the police and have them follow us."

"How could we get an invitation? They know who we are."

Bailey smiled smugly. "I'm a hairdresser, remember? You'd be surprised at what a difference a change in hair color and style can make. While we wait for your face and ribs to heal, you can let your beard grow, deepen your tan, buy tinted contact lenses." She stopped to study him. "That body will be tough to hide. I'll really have to do a good job on your hair. Maybe a perm." She grinned. "I promise not to take a picture of you in curlers."

Steele grimaced at the thought, but he couldn't deny her idea had merit. "Lana would know my voice. I'm not sure she's an unwilling participant in all this."

"I'll give you voice lessons. Bonnie and I did a twin act when we were small. You'd have to practice until it was second nature, though. No mistakes."

Steele rubbed his jaw, considering her plan and trying to find holes in it. There was only one. "I like it," he said, "but I have one condition. I do it alone."

"No way!" Bailey leapt to her feet and stood over him, as though to intimidate him. "If you're alone, they'll look at you more closely. Your size could make them suspicious. If you're with me, I can draw a lot of attention away from you. I'll dress to the nines and play the part of your pampered plaything. Together, they'll see us as a couple, not as individuals." She stopped, out of breath from talking so fast.

"Bailey," he said gently, taking her hands in his, "if you're right about that club, your husband lost his life because of what he saw. How can you ask me to risk yours?"

Slowly Bailey lowered herself to her knees in front of him. "Because," she began, then drew a deep breath.

"Cliff and Ron weren't the only ones in the truck." She swallowed heavily. "Travis," her voice broke, and her light eyes shimmered with a veil of tears, "my four-year-old son was in it, too."

4

STEELE PULLED BAILEY into his lap and cradled her against his chest. Her weight pressed against his sore ribs, but he would've endured pain ten times worse if he could ease hers. To lose Kevin, to never again hear him cry, "Daddy" when he walked into the house—he couldn't bear to think about it. Just the threat of his son being kidnapped had sent him flying from his home and across the country.

How could he refuse Bailey this chance for vengeance? Her scheme was brilliant, but risky. If anything went wrong, as a woman, she'd have neither the strength nor speed for escape. She'd slow him down and endanger both their lives. Somehow, he had to persuade her to let him work alone.

Not now, though.

She clung to him, her slender frame shuddering, her tears warm and wet against the hollow of his neck. He massaged the ridges of her spine and dropped soft kisses on the top of her head, but he'd never felt more helpless. Nothing he could say or do would give her back her son. He had no words of comfort to give.

He didn't even have a handkerchief to offer her when she calmed. "Excuse me," she mumbled, slipping from his grasp and stumbling into the house. The German shepherd rose and eyed Steele, as if expecting him to follow her.

"She might like to be alone," Steele said, thinking aloud and not sure what to do.

Max's stare didn't waver. Unmoving, Steele stared back. Max barked, a short, commanding sound, then trotted to the kitchen door. Turning his head toward Steele, he again gave him an impatient look.

"Okay, you know her better than I do." Steele stood and let the dog in the house. Max led him through a hallway to a closed door. Behind it, he could hear water running.

When the water stopped and the door opened, he stepped back. Bailey's pinkened face and swollen eyes shone with water. Her shoulders were straight, though, and her chin uplifted. She saw Max, knelt and hugged him.

For an odd, irrational moment, Steele felt jealous of the dog. She seemed to find a comfort in the animal that he hadn't been able to give her. When she stood and faced him, her eyes seemed clearer and she smiled wanly.

"You think you'll run out of tears, but you never do," she said in a low voice, then dropped her gaze and led the way to the kitchen. "Are you hungry?" She lifted the lid of a Crock-Pot, and the tantalizing aroma of a stew filled the air.

"Famished," he admitted. "What can I do to help?"

"Not a thing, just take a seat."

He sat down at the table in the windowed bay and watched her while she fed Max. The dog licked her cheek when she set his bowl on the floor. Petting him, she assured him she was all right. She straightened and glanced at Steele.

"Max misses them, too," she said simply.

Cliff and Travis, Steele filled in the names rather than ask. No wonder she seemed so close to the dog; he was all she had left of her family.

She brought two bowls of a beef, carrot and potato stew to the table. "Tell me more about Lana," she said, sitting on the opposite side of the table. She slid the larger bowl of stew toward him, but didn't touch hers.

"We were high-school sweethearts." Guessing she needed conversation to distance herself from her emotions, Steele chose to start at the beginning. "She went by Karen, then. She didn't switch to her middle name, Lana, until later." He paused, pushing back the anger the name always stirred within him, and tried a bite of the steaming stew. The beef was tender and the vegetables flavorful. He complimented her, then went on with his story.

"She was a sophomore, transferred in halfway through my senior year. Almost six feet tall with long blond hair, she caught my eye right away." He smiled, this memory bittersweet. She'd returned his open stare with a level one of her own, one that said, Don't mess with me.

He'd already won the national Mr. Teenage America bodybuilding contest and had his pick of most of the girls in the school, but he'd wanted Karen. Karen, with a chip on her shoulder a mile wide. The daughter of domestic servants who lived in furnished quarters on their employer's estate, she'd rated a zero on the school social scale.

Unlike her, he was on the same economic level as the other students, but he knew what it was like to be on the fringe. His father had earned his money in the boxing ring, not quite on par with upper-crust corporate executives.

While he talked, he saw Bailey lift her spoon to her mouth. "I was doing well on the professional body-building circuit when Karen graduated, and we got married," he continued, pleased to see he'd diverted her attention enough to restore her appetite. "When we weren't on the road, we worked in my dad's gym—Karen taught aerobics—and lived with him, too. He loved her like a daughter and liked having a woman around the house. My mother died when I was five, and he never remarried." The thought of his father brought another smile to his lips. "I was born in a run-down neighborhood in Bridgeport, Connecticut. Each time Dad rose in the boxing ranks, though, we moved into a nicer place, finally settling in Westport. Whenever we looked at a house, his first consideration was where he'd hang my mother's portrait. It's over the mantel in my living room now."

"Can you remember her?" Bailey asked. They both finished eating and set their bowls on the floor for Max to lick.

"Vague impressions of someone soft and sweet-smelling. She was such a lady, Dad always said he couldn't believe she'd married him, that she'd be waiting for him when he got home. After she died, he sometimes felt like he'd dreamed her. Then we'd sit on the couch and look at her portrait together." He blinked rapidly, his throat tightening.

Bailey reached for his hand and took it in both of hers. "He's dead?" she asked.

He nodded, embarrassed by his show of emotion. "Last year," he rasped. "I still miss him." Afraid he'd break down if he continued to see the understanding sympathy in her eyes, he swallowed and looked down at their hands. Although her fingers were long, slender and fragile, their grip was strong.

Admiration for her flooded through him. She looked soft and vulnerable, but he'd seen how strong willed she was. She'd survived the loss of her husband and child, yet still had compassion for him, a stranger she'd found hurt on the beach.

He wanted her. Wanted to kiss and caress her. Wanted to fill her sad emptiness with the heat of his living, breathing body.

He withdrew his hand from hers. He was in no condition to make love to a woman and doubted she'd welcome such an advance. "Anyway, Karen and I were the perfect couple. Tall, blond and athletic." He grinned mockingly. "When I was twenty-four, I won the Mr. Olympia title. I'd reached the top, so we decided to start a family. Everything went downhill from there."

Bailey's light eyes widened, and her lips parted with surprise.

"Pregnancy didn't agree with Karen. She was sick a lot and hated watching her body swell. When Kevin was born, she told me I owed her. She wanted her own house and wanted it in Las Vegas." Reaching the unpleasant part of his memories, he talked faster, wanting to get it over with.

"We'd gone there on vacation for her twenty-first birthday. I didn't particularly like it, but, if she'd asked for the moon, I would've tried to give it to her. I hooked up with the athletic facilities at a resort and coached when I wasn't competing. Karen hired a nanny for Kevin and got a job in a chorus line."

He looked past Bailey, no longer seeing her. "I worked days, she worked nights. She changed her name to Lana

Stevens and turned into a stranger. I didn't know she'd fallen in love with the roulette wheel until she woke me one morning with a shower of cash. I thought she was using her own money and passing time between shows— until my checks bounced. She'd hit a 'small' losing streak." He scowled. "We were talking over two-thousand bucks. I made her promise to stop gambling."

He laughed humorlessly. "She broke that promise. Repeatedly. I contacted Gamblers Anonymous, where I was advised to cut off her funds. By paying her debts, I was what they call an 'enabler.' To help her, I needed to make her face what she was doing. She was furious when I told her I'd taken her name off all my accounts, even our credit cards, which she'd run up to the limit on the machines scattered so conveniently throughout the casinos."

"Compulsive gamblers are like alcoholics," Bailey commented.

"Worse," Steele corrected. "An alcoholic has periods of sobriety. A compulsive gambler is never free of the obsession. She couldn't even spend a full day off with Kevin or me. And they're *liars*." He spat out the word. "She'd say she was going to the grocery store, but hours later I'd find her in some backstreet casino. She'd take out loans and skip payments, then the banks would try to bill me. I should've left her sooner, but . . ."

"You still loved her," Bailey concluded when his voice trailed away.

"She told me she was pregnant. By that time, we argued more often than we made love, but I believed her. She promised to give her notice at work, then I left on a road trip. When I got home, she told me she'd miscarried. Even cried big, crocodile tears." Angry at his own gullibility, he slammed his fist on the table. Max jumped out of his sleep at their feet. Bailey soothed the dog, while Steele went on blindly. Caught up in his memories, he couldn't stop.

"I called her doctor the next day. Maybe I suspected something, I don't know..." He shrugged. "He didn't know a damn thing about a pregnancy, much less a miscarriage. She tried to give me a song and dance about going to a different doctor, but I didn't want to hear it.

"Not long after that my Dad called to ask why I hadn't asked him for a loan instead of withdrawing money from the trust fund he'd set up for Kevin." He squeezed his eyes closed, the pain of that day embedded in his soul. "She'd gone through my papers and found the certificate. And forged my name."

He opened his eyes and again focused on Bailey. "I hung up the phone and packed. I took Kevin to a friend's house and waited for *Lana* to come home. Karen, as far as I was concerned, no longer existed." He laid both hands on the table, opening and closing his fists. Bailey slipped her hands in his.

Calming, he continued. "When I told her I wanted a divorce and was taking Kevin back to Connecticut with me, all she asked was if she could keep the house." He shook his head. "I gave her the house, a car and money on the condition she grant me full custody of Kevin. She *sold* her son. She hasn't seen him once in the three years since the divorce."

"Deep down, she knew she was sick," Bailey said, "and Kevin was better off with you."

Sympathy had tinted her light eyes again, but this time it was sympathy for Lana, Steele realized with amazement. "She's *weak!*" he exploded, jerking his hands from hers. "Because of her, Kevin is in danger. If I give in to these thugs, they'll keep lending her money, and Kevin will never be safe again."

"I don't mean you should pay them," Bailey said quickly. "Like Cliff, my father was a dealer. Both of them said they could spot the compulsive gamblers. Winning is a rush, a high, for anyone, but some people get addicted to it. Just like drug addicts, they'll do anything to get their fix. The more they lose, the more desperate they become." She shook her head sadly. "It sounds like Lana would be exactly the type of gambler the private party Cliff worked would attract. Out for the big win and willing to risk everything."

"Including her son," Steele added grimly.

"I'm sure she thought he was safe with you," Bailey said charitably.

Steele scowled, refusing to think Lana had any such consideration.

"If I'm right," she continued, "and there is a connection between Lana's disappearance and that club in the mountains, my plan will put those responsible in jail. Kevin won't be threatened again. It's going to cost money, though, and you'll have to play the role of a high-stakes gambler, the type of person you have reason to hate. Are you sure you can do it?"

"There isn't anything I won't do to protect Kevin."

"What's your best game?"

Steele looked at her blankly.

"Roulette, like Lana? Craps? Blackjack? Poker?"

"None of them," he confessed. "When we went to Vegas on vacation, I wound up watching Karen. She was like a kid in a candy store." He winced, remembering how her eyes had sparkled, how she'd laughed and clapped her hands and asked him to blow on the dice for luck. Neither of them had had an inkling of how her excitement would lead to obsession. "I thought she was cute."

"We'll make you a blackjack player, then. Cliff loved to study all the angles of the game and taught me."

"You've got a deal." Steele tried, but couldn't manage, to stifle a yawn.

Bailey glanced at the clock. "You need your rest, and I have to work in the morning. Let's call it a night."

STEELE OBJECTED to taking her bed, but Bailey insisted. Her rattan couch was too short for him, as were the bunk beds in the other bedroom. Still arguing, he stood in the doorway to her room while she selected clothes for work, then pulled lingerie and a nightgown from a drawer.

"We could always share," Steele suggested, eyeing the tropical print of the satiny chemise and wrap she tossed over the dress on her arm.

"I don't think so." Bailey tried to sound stern, but a smile softened her rejection. Steele's light attempts at flirtation flattered, rather than threatened her.

"Another time, perhaps?" he added, when she passed him on her way from the bedroom to the bathroom.

"Sleep well," she said, avoiding an answer.

"I'll dream of you dressed in that outfit," he called through the closed bathroom door.

Bailey laughed, and a smile lingered on her lips as she hung her dress on the shower rod, slipped into her brightly colored nightclothes and prepared for bed.

Her instincts about Steele had been right, she mused. He was a good man, compassionate and kind. She felt as if she'd known him for years instead of one short day.

A result, no doubt, of the confidences they'd shared. Like soldiers in combat or strangers caught in disaster, they'd formed an immediate bond. What she had to remember, though, was such a bond dissolved when the danger was over.

She knew better than to count on the future; the room where she'd sleep was irrefutable evidence. Travis's bedroom.

Bailey let Max in the bedroom and closed the door behind them, without bothering to turn on the light. She headed unerringly for the bunk beds and plucked the stuffed rabbit from the pillow of the lower bunk. Clutching it to her breasts, she crawled between the sheets. She didn't need light to see her son's toybox overflowing in one corner or the baseball players dotting the bedspreads on the bunk beds and smiling from posters on the walls.

Max nosed her cheek gently, then settled by the side of the bed. Bailey reached down and petted his silky ears. "It's just you and me, Max," she whispered in what had become a nightly ritual. His quiet, comforting presence had seen her through many long, dark hours.

She hadn't told Steele how often she escaped the loneliness of her queen-size bed by sleeping in this room, her last tie to her son's short life. She hadn't told Bonnie, either, but she didn't have to. Bonnie knew, which was why she nagged at her to give away Travis's toys and redecorate. But she couldn't bring herself to do it.

Maybe, if her suspicions proved correct, and she saw the people responsible for the deaths of her son and husband punished, she'd be able to accept her loss and go forward with her life.

Maybe.

STEELE WOKE to an empty house. A note in the bathroom told him that Bailey had gone to work, but that Max was in the yard and might like to come in to visit. She reminded him not to shave, since he'd need a beard for his disguise, and asked him to remain indoors and keep the curtains drawn until she returned. Her neighbors, she explained, might think he was a prowler and call the police. While he understood the need to keep a low profile, he chafed at the confinement. He wasn't used to inactivity, and daytime television bored him.

On the way to the kitchen, where her note had told him coffee waited, he noticed a door, closed yesterday, now open. He glanced inside and recognized a child's bedroom.

The bottom bunk bed was unmade, as if a child had hurried to school and would return in the afternoon. But Travis, he knew, would never return.

Two baseball gloves, one a miniature of the other, hung from pegs on a wall. Thoughts of the too-short lives of the father and son who'd used them drew him across the room. He lifted the small one from its peg; the leather was stiff from lack of use. His heart contracting painfully, he put it back and turned away, his glance landing on framed photographs on adjacent bookshelves.

The first showed Bailey, dressed in bridal white, smiling up at her tuxedo-clad husband. Cliff was medium-height and lean with brown hair and eyes. Looking at the photo, he felt a flash of relief. In no way did Steele resemble him.

In the second photograph, Bailey was in a hospital bed, a bald, red-faced newborn in her arms. Travis was several months old in the next picture and had sprouted tufts of Bailey's black hair. Giggling at the camera, his brown eyes wide, he lay naked on a wide bed. Other photographs depicted family gatherings at birthdays, holidays and Bonnie's wedding. Her husband was fair and more solidly built than Bailey's.

The last picture stood next to a row of photo albums on a separate shelf. Travis wore his baseball glove, still much too large for him despite its reduced size. He held it up to his father proudly, a ball nestled in the glove's palm.

Steele could see the scene all too clearly: Cliff lobbing the ball directly into his son's glove and praising him for his "great catch" while his wife captured the moment on film.

A lump rose in his throat, and he turned away. He stared at the unmade bed, unseeing, then blinked. A stuffed rabbit lay atop the pillow, incongruous against the baseball motif of the sheets and comforter.

Picking it up, he saw the fur on one side of it was worn away, an eye was missing and an ear torn. Had it been in such poor condition when Travis died? Or had over a year of Bailey's grieving damaged it? Gently, he set the rabbit back where he'd found it.

He couldn't help wishing Bailey would choose to sleep with something larger and warmer.

Namely, him.

BAILEY LAUGHED through her morning at the salon. Her customers laughed with her, and her tips soared. Her good mood, she knew, resulted from the release of tears and the knowledge that, at last, she was going to pursue her suspicions.

When she met her sister for lunch, though, she led her to think her high spirits rose from a romantic interest in Steele and his decision to go to the police.

Neither was a total lie, which allowed her to be more convincing. She *was* attracted to Steele—not that she intended to do anything about it—and they *would* go to the authorities—as soon as they'd found the casino in the Dead Mountains and confirmed her theory of crooked gambling.

"Be careful, Bails," Bonnie warned when she'd completed her explanation.

Afraid her sister's psychic antenna had detected her deception, Bailey almost choked on a mouthful of chef's salad.

"You're like a pendulum swinging from one extreme to the other," Bonnie continued. "Slow down. Yeah, the guy's a hunk, but how much do you really know about him?"

Relieved to realize Bonnie was being her usual, cautious self, Bailey swallowed more easily. "I have good judgment when it comes to men. I fixed you up with Ron, remember?"

Bonnie smiled. "You tricked me, as I recall. You were so in love with Cliff, I thought you'd forgotten you had a sister. I finally got an invitation to dinner with the new bride only to find myself stuck with the bridegroom's softball buddy for a blind date!"

"And you never looked at another man." Bailey's smug grin faded when Bonnie sighed and glanced away instead of laughing. "I'm sorry," she said quickly, reaching across the table to squeeze her sister's hand.

Bonnie shrugged away the apology. "It's nice to remember, even if it hurts." Summoning a bright smile, she changed the subject, but Bailey's mood darkened. Her sister's husband had been as innocent a passenger in Cliff's truck as Travis.

Bonnie kicked herself for dimming her sister's unusually good humor and asked more questions about Steele. Bailey poured out the story of his childhood and marriage. Familiar with the pitfalls of gambling, Bonnie found the tale believable and warmed toward Steele.

The mix of feminine pride and pleasure in Bailey's eyes when she described his lighthearted efforts to flirt with her swept away any lingering reservations about him. "I'm envious," Bonnie admitted. "None of my dates make me feel the way Steele obviously affects you."

"Is this the same woman who warned me to be careful ten minutes ago?" Bailey asked, her smile teasing.

"That was before you told me more about him," Bonnie retorted. "I like the way he tried to help Lana and didn't give up on her until she spent money intended for their son's future." Finishing her tuna sandwich, she pushed away the plate. "Most of all, I like the sparkle he puts in your eyes. I haven't seen you this happy in a long time. To be honest, you scared me with your talk of murder yesterday. If you'll feel better, go with Steele to the police. Tell them your suspicions and ask them to investigate the club in the Dead Mountains."

When Bonnie saw Bailey's gaze falter, she assumed her reference to their talk the previous day saddened her. She hurried on, intent on making her point. "In the meantime, put the past behind you. Give Steele a chance. Nothing will bring Travis or Cliff back. Make a new life for yourself."

"I just met the guy," Bailey complained, squirming in her seat, "and now you're trying to marry me off!"

She was pushing her too hard, Bonnie realized. "Hey, I've been dating and know what's out there," she said to lighten the mood. "So far, I've found nothing but safe and boring Mama's boys or heavy-breathing Casanovas. How can I let you pass up a man who combines brains and charm with *that* body?"

Bailey laughed. Satisfied she'd restored her sister's good mood, Bonnie signaled the waitress for their check. In a scant twenty-four hours, Steele had put life back into her sister. She hoped Bailey would, for once, take her advice. In the meantime, she'd do everything in her power to help the relationship along—and keep hoping she could find one for herself.

BORED OUT OF HIS skull by the time Bailey walked in her front door, Steele greeted her as happily as Max wagged his tail.

"Ready for your first blackjack lesson?" she asked, handing him one of her grocery bags to free a hand to pet Max.

"Sure," he agreed, envying Max her touch. She led the way to the kitchen. He settled for enjoying his view of her. Her wavy hair was caught up in a ponytail, and she wore a short, lilac-and-white-striped, tunic dress loosely belted over her hips, with white sandals laced over her shapely ankles. "Better yet, is there a strip version like in poker?"

She set her grocery bag on the counter and turned to him with a reproving smile. "You're an incorrigible flirt, aren't you?"

"No." He'd barely looked at a woman since he'd left Lana. "You inspire me."

"Right." She rolled her eyes and swung away from him to unpack the food. "What would you like for dinner?"

"I found some chicken breasts in the freezer and thawed them. They're marinating in a teriyaki sauce. I thought I'd grill them."

"You cook?"

He grinned at her surprise. "I get by. I have a cleaning service three days a week, but I don't believe in turning my son over to hired help."

"Good for you."

Her approval warmed him. "By the way, I'd like to call him, but I should use a pay phone." The need to hear his son's voice had grown throughout the day. Bailey's loss made him more aware of how abruptly a life could end.

"You can use mine."

He shook his head. "Calls can be traced. For all I know, my friends are being watched. I don't want you involved."

She arched an eyebrow. "I *am* involved."

"Anymore than you already are." When her eyebrow rose higher, Steele cursed his clumsy tongue.

"What exactly is that supposed to mean?" She crossed her arms beneath her breasts and tapped one foot.

Lovely, Steele thought, wishing he could close the space separating them and kiss her until she forgot her question.

When he didn't answer, Bailey came to him. "Don't even think of trying to cut me out of this." She jabbed his bare chest with her index finger. After locating her washer and dryer, he'd cleaned and donned his jeans, but he'd removed the bandage on his ribs to shower and thrown away the shirt she'd cut open.

"You need me more than I need you," she continued, her ponytail bobbing with each jab of her finger. "You not only don't know how to gamble, you don't have a car or clothes. Without me, you'd also have to go to a salon to change your appearance and risk being seen."

"Okay, I see your point." Steele lifted his hands to signal surrender. He'd have to learn how to play blackjack and complete his disguise before persuading her to allow him to continue with the plan alone. "Speaking of clothes, I need to get mine from my hotel. And I've got a rental car to take care of, too."

Bailey's anger dissipated while she considered his problem. "Your hotel might be watched. If you check out, they'll know you're still alive."

He nodded, having already considered this possibility. "I tried to keep a low profile by flying into Phoenix and renting a car. I'll tell the hotel clerk I've had a run of bad luck and have to go home early, then return the car to the airport, buy a ticket and get lost in the crowd. When I'm sure I'm not being followed, I'll rent another car and come back to Laughlin."

"I'll take my car and meet you at the airport," Bailey corrected. Steele scowled his disagreement, but she ignored him. "We can shop for our disguises while we're in Phoenix rather than risk being seen in the local stores."

"Don't you have to work?"

"Yes, but I can trade shifts and get some extra days off. While I'm at work tomorrow, I'll buy us some wigs too. We can rehearse our roles while we're away." Steele grimaced, but Bailey again ignored him.

"If you duck into a bathroom at the airport, put on your wig and change clothes, you can be sure to ditch anyone following you. I'll get a shirt for you, while I'm at it. You can't walk through a hotel lobby. . ." her gaze lowered, lingering on his bare chest, and her voice faltered ". . . like that." She stepped back, as if suddenly uncomfortable with their proximity.

Pleased to see she wasn't as unaware of him as she pretended, Steele grinned. "Anytime you'd like to touch as well as look, feel free," he drawled, opening his arms in invitation.

Bailey spun away from him. "Where's this chicken?" she asked, opening the refrigerator. "Do you want to start the coals while I shower and change?"

Soundless in his bare feet, Steele followed her across the kitchen. "No need to make it a cold shower on my account," he whispered in her ear.

Swiveling to face him, Bailey jammed the cold plastic container of chicken into his solar plexus. "You're the one who needs to cool off," she retorted and marched from the kitchen.

5

THE WATER THAT PASSED for cold in the summer months was tepid, adding to Bailey's aggravation. She needed a shower icy enough to turn her numb. Acknowledging Steele's appeal was one thing; longing to trace every line and curve on his muscular chest was another. She never wanted to feel *anything* again. Not desire, not love, not even happiness because she wouldn't risk the sorrow she knew lurked around the corner from it.

Remembering how she'd misled her sister at lunch and how earnestly Bonnie had advised her to give Steele a chance, she suppressed a trace of guilt. She'd never lied to her twin before. But she'd had no choice. Her sister wouldn't understand. Bonnie had a fatherless daughter to consider, a reason to gamble on life and love again.

Bailey, however, had lost her child as well as her husband and wanted revenge, not a new life or love. If Bonnie knew her plans, she'd not only try to dissuade her, she'd worry about her.

Mentally promising to apologize in the future, Bailey stepped from the shower and returned her mind to the problem of dealing with her attraction to Steele. She'd give him an old shirt of Cliff's to wear, she decided. With the tempting expanse of his chest covered, she'd keep her mind on their plan, where it belonged.

"You'll need something to wear to a pay phone," she said when she found Steele sitting on the glider on the back porch. She tossed the white T-shirt in his face to end his leisurely survey of her shorts-clad legs. "We'll go as soon as it's dark."

"Will you help me put it on?" he asked, deftly catching the shirt before it dropped into his lap. "It still hurts to lift my arms over my head." He slid his hands through the short sleeves, then raised his arms to shoulder-height.

Reluctantly, she stepped in front of him and worked the sleeves to his biceps. The knit fabric stretched, but refused to slide over the rounded muscles. "We'll have to cut the sleeves out," she said and hurried into the house for scissors.

When she returned, he'd left the shirt on the glider and risen to check the chicken on the grill. The muscles of his back rippled as he wielded the spatula. Bailey attacked the shirt. Since the sleeves were too small, she figured the rest of it would be, too, so she snipped out extra-large armholes and cut off the binding around the neck.

Steele laughed when he turned and she held it up. "Why bother?" he asked. "I'll attract more attention in this than I would if I was shirtless."

Once she had it on him, Bailey was inclined to agree. The armholes she'd cut split down to his waist, inviting her to slide her hands inside and stroke his warm flesh. As if to tempt her further, he unsnapped the waistband of his jeans to tuck in the shirt without turning his back to her.

"It hides the worst of your bruises," she said in a forced tone of voice, "and I'll take you by boat to a marina. People will think you've been fishing and camping. You won't stand out like you would at a convenience store or gas station."

"If you say so." He glanced at her as though aware that the shirt was intended more for her peace of mind than to make him less conspicuous. He certainly didn't rush to refasten his jeans.

They ate, then left at dusk. Bailey waited in the boat at the park dock, while Steele made his call. The water lapped at the pilings on the wharf, a dog barked in the distance but, tuned for trouble, she heard nothing else.

Steele hadn't been gone long, though, when the sound of rapidly approaching footsteps brought her to her feet. She peered over the dock and saw him running toward her. Ducking back into the boat, she started the engine, ready to race away the moment he reached her.

As soon as he jumped into the boat, she pushed away from the pier, slipped behind the wheel and roared away. Steele stumbled to the seat beside her.

"Are you trying to kill us?" he yelled. "Slow down!"

"But they'll catch us!"

"Who?" He looked behind him.

Bailey kept her attention directed forward. Not many boats were out this time of night, but a collision at her speed would be fatal.

Steele pressed his lips to her ear. "Look for yourself. Nobody's after us!"

Bailey let up on the throttle and twisted around in her seat to look behind them. The moon was full, bright enough to illuminate another boat, even if its lights were out. "Then why were you running?" she asked, turning back to him.

He grinned with embarrassment. "Kevin was half-asleep when he came to the phone. I didn't keep him, but I was so happy to hear his voice and, after being cooped up all day, it felt good to run." He paused. "I didn't mean to frighten you. Forgive me?"

Letting the engine idle, Bailey stared at him. The light of the moon streamed through the small cabin windows, silvering his blond hair and highlighting the straight line of his nose, the flat planes of his cheeks and the firm square of his chin. She'd thought their lives were in danger all because this big, handsome dope had been so overjoyed to hear his son's voice, he'd run back to the boat like an exuberant child?

"You scared me to death!" she yelled, her nerves stretched paper-thin and her heart still galloping with adrenaline. "I could've run us into a piling, or, or..." Words failed her. Laughing, she rained featherlight blows on his head and shoulders, while he faked loud moans and pretended to cower in front of her.

Abruptly he caught her hands and pulled her into his lap. Bending his head, he silenced her laughter with a kiss. Bailey let her eyes drift closed and held very still, as the unfamiliar contours of his lips molded to hers. The heat of the desert night seemed to wrap around her... desire stirred and seeped through her veins...

But something was wrong.

She felt massive muscle against her breasts instead of sinewy strength and missed the faint scent of a tangy after-shave.

He wasn't Cliff.

Cliff was dead.

She slipped off Steele's lap. "I can't," she said softly. She returned to her seat, put the boat back into gear and guided it toward home.

She felt, rather than saw Steele study her. "Three *is* a crowd," he murmured.

"Four's even worse. What about Lana?" she added, thinking of the tenderness in his voice when he'd referred to his wife as Karen.

"No." The quiet intensity of his denial drew her gaze to his face. "I have no feelings left for a woman who chose the roulette wheel over her son."

"What about hate?"

A muscle rippled in his cheek. He jerked his head in a nod.

Steele's response told her he was no more free of the memory of his wife than she was of her husband's but, rather than argue with him, she turned her attention back to the river. It stretched before them, as dark and empty as her heart.

THE MOMENT BAILEY and Steele walked into her home, Bailey claimed exhaustion and disappeared with Max into her son's bedroom. Knowing what a reminder of her past the room was, Steele tried to coax her out to no avail. His blackjack lessons could wait, she called through the closed door. His ribs would take weeks to heal.

He'd moved too fast. Disgusted with himself, Steele flopped onto the couch and tried to watch television. He shouldn't have kissed her. Her marriage, unlike his, had been a happy one, cut short by tragedy rather than by choice.

The moment of shared laughter had seemed so right, though . . .

He switched off the television and paced the small living room. Despite the spacious effect of the sand-colored carpeting, ivory drapes and pastel furniture cushions, the walls seemed to close in on him.

Bailey had loved another man in this house and borne his child, then lost them both. How could he fight such memories?

Before she'd withdrawn from his kiss, he'd sensed a glimmer of response, though. He'd have to woo her with patience, he decided, and slowly accustom her to his touch.

But he didn't feel patient, not with only a door separating them. Striding through the kitchen and into the night, he jogged down the hill to the river and back, until his laboring lungs knocked against his sore ribs and made him stop.

But he still didn't feel very patient.

"YOU'RE GOING TO spoil me," Bailey said when she returned from work the next day and found that Steele had again planned dinner. Determined to keep her distance from him, she evaded the kiss he tried to plant on her cheek by bending to greet Max, then breezing past him.

"It's the least I can do. I'm eating you out of house and home." Steele followed her into the living room. "And you won't take any money for groceries."

"You can pay for our meals during our shopping trip to Phoenix. I've got two days off. We can leave in the morning. I made hotel reservations and appointments for us to be fitted with tinted contact lenses. Bonnie's going to take care of Max. Is there anything I forgot?"

"One room or two?"

"Two." Shooting him an exasperated glance, she set the shopping bag she carried on the couch and pulled a shirt out of it. Couldn't the man take no for an answer? "I scoured the town for a T-shirt as big as a sheet for you to wear to the hotel in the morning."

"I think I've been insulted." Steele muttered and assumed a woeful expression.

"You have," she assured him, unable to repress a smile. "We'll have to find one of those 'big men' stores in Phoenix. We can buy clothes that make you look like you're running to fat to disguise your muscles."

He shuddered graphically. "A bodybuilder's nightmare."

"You'll still look handsome." She patted his stubbled cheek. "Especially when your beard grows in."

"Oh, yeah?" He grasped her waist and pulled her close. "How handsome?"

Mistake, Bailey thought as she stared at the bare chest in front of her nose. She shouldn't have touched him, but his humor had relaxed her guard. "Oh, very," she assured him with a lightness she didn't feel. Twisting from his grasp, she reached into the shopping bag again. "And you'll look even better in this." She held up a short wig.

"Red?" he asked, grimacing.

"Auburn. I thought it would match your beard." Actually she'd recalled the reddish-blond color of the hair sprinkled on his chest, but she wouldn't admit it. "I'll trim it to suit your face. No one will guess it's not real." She dropped the wig on the couch and pulled sunglasses from the bag. "I bought the wraparound style to hide your black eye. Don't wear them until you change clothes and put on your wig at the airport. Try them and make sure they fit." Steele obeyed, and she laughed. "You look like Arnold Schwarzenegger in the first *Terminator* movie!"

"*Hasta la vista*, baby," he growled in Schwarzenegger's Austrian accent.

"That was the second movie."

"Yeah, but I'd rather be the good guy sent to protect Linda Hamilton." He reached for her, but she snatched her shopping bag and twirled away.

"I'll change clothes, then get my scissors and give your wig a haircut on the deck. We can decide on our new identities, too."

"I can hardly wait."

Laughing at the lack of enthusiasm in his voice, Bailey picked up the bag and left the room. If he felt a wig diminished his masculinity, she could imagine his reaction when she dyed and permed his hair. If their plan worked, though, their disguises had to be foolproof.

She sobered while she tucked her hair into the wig she'd bought for herself. To play her role as Steele's mistress convincingly, she'd have to touch more than his cheek. She stared at her new blond image in the mirror.

She could and would do it. Steele would play the high-stakes gambler to protect his son, and she would play an immoral woman to see those who'd killed her family punished.

Carla, she named herself, reaching for her cosmetics. Carla Canfield would coo, cuddle up and cling to Steele.

WHEN SHE STEPPED onto the porch, Steele was in the yard, tossing a Frisbee to Max. "What do you think?" she called from the railing. His gaze caressed her legs, lingered on the tight fit of her cutoff jeans, then slowed still more when it reached her bare midriff and halter top.

"I'm Carla Canfield," she announced, once his visual tour finally reached her shoulder-length, blond wig. His heated examination of her body increased the breathiness in the Marilyn Monroe voice she'd chosen for her new personality. "I'll be meeting you at the airport to-morrow."

"Dressed like that?" He climbed the steps to the deck, while Max trotted toward his water bowl in the shade.

Bailey shook her head, allowing the straight hair of the wig to fall across one eye. Acting came naturally to her, since she'd performed onstage as a child, and she'd chosen her clothes as the character of Carla would have.

"I'll have to dress up a little more, but I'm sure I can find something else in prim little Bailey's closet to turn a man's head."

"Bailey does that without trying." He stopped and stood before her.

"Bailey isn't a rich man's kept woman," she responded, determined to remain in character. She ran a long fingernail, now painted red instead of her usual pink, down the middle of his chest. "I am."

Steele sucked in his breath. "Carla's more free with her favors." He lifted her arms and placed them around his neck, the look in his eyes challenging her to take the charade further.

"Only with men who can afford her," she purred.

Steele shifted their positions so he could lean against the railing, then dropped his hands to her hips and pulled her into the V between his legs. She felt the stirring in his groin press against her softer abdomen and tensed as the tips of her breasts stiffened against his chest in response.

Steele wasn't acting, she realized nervously, and neither was her body.

"I make a comfortable living, but I'm not rich enough for a woman like Carla." His eyes were heavy-lidded and focused on her mouth.

"But you're, um..." Bailey struggled to think "...Matt, ah, Logan. How did you make your money, Matt?"

Steele ran his hands up and down her sides, tracing the curve of waist and hip. "Why don't you tell me?"

Bailey lowered her gaze and rested her forehead against his chest. She should step back, away from him. Steele's flesh was warm. *She* was warm. Too warm. And, yet, she savored the languorous heat.

"You have to decide," she mumbled. "Something you can talk intelligently about." She had to get used to his touch, she reminded herself, to play the role of his mistress.

"Hmm..." Steele moved his hands to her shoulder blades, massaging the tight, tense muscles. "Let's say my daddy's rich." The faint, twangy Texas drawl he put on his words brought her head up.

She nodded approval, but advised, "A little deeper."

"He started out in oil and diversified early," he continued, lowering his baritone voice into a bass. "Managers attend to the details. I keep an eye on the investment portfolio."

"When you're not running around with women and spending the money," Bailey added, dropping her head back to his chest.

His fingers traced the path of her spine. "You got it, honey."

"And you met me in Vegas. I was a cocktail waitress, who brought you luck at the blackjack tables."

"And other places." He slid his hands from her hips and cupped the curves of her behind. Thrown out of character by the intimate grasp, she glared at him. A sensual half smile on his lips, he cocked an eyebrow and tightened his grip.

Speechless, she twisted her arms behind her back and tugged at his wrists. Quick to take advantage of her outthrust breasts, Steele bent and nuzzled at the cleft exposed by the halter top. The warm, moist glide of his tongue on her sensitive flesh stilled her fruitless struggle. Bailey dropped her arms to her sides and moaned, then shivered deliciously when his breath fanned the dampened skin. Steele raised his head, but his hands continued to knead her buttocks.

"It's Bailey, I want, not Carla. Who am I holding?"

His words shattered her sensual haze. She stepped away and set up one of the folding lawn chairs leaning against the side of the house. "Sit," she ordered, pulling off her wig and shaking out her hair. She simply wasn't ready to deal with the feelings he aroused in her.

Steele sat, but groaned audibly. She looked at him in surprise. "Bailey's even harder to resist than Carla," he explained, eyeing the black waves cascading past her shoulders.

"Oh, shut up," she snapped. Confused and irritable, she was in no mood for his seductive compliments. She picked up his wig and moved behind him.

He swiveled to face her. "What's the matter?" His innocent expression infuriated her still more.

"We need to establish some rules, here." She turned his face away and jammed the wig on his head. "I may be playing the part of your mistress, but that doesn't mean you can..." she drew a deep breath "...take liberties with my body."

He jumped to his feet. "And what the hell do you think you were doing with mine?"

"*I* didn't do anything that couldn't be done in public."

"You were all over me!"

"That's what I'm supposed to do!"

"How the hell am I supposed to react? I happen to be a man, not a chunk of rock!"

"You should react like a playboy who knows women like me are a dime a dozen. You—"

"No, Bailey," he interrupted, his voice serious rather than angry. "No way could I pretend there's another woman like you on this planet."

Bailey felt her mouth open, then close. She shook her head, refusing to be diverted by his flattery. "We're discussing Carla, who is no more to Matt Logan than an expensive toy. You treat her as such." Steele started to grin. "And since we'll be performing in public, even if we're rehearsing—"

"Rehearsing?" he interrupted again. "Is that what we were doing?"

"I wasn't wearing a wig in this heat for my health." She paused, unsuccessfully trying to glare his grin into submission. "Even if we're rehearsing in private, you have to remain within the bounds of propriety."

"Which are?" he drawled, his grin widening.

She rolled her eyes. "You know perfectly well what I mean."

He leaned back against the railing and folded his arms across his chest. "No, I'm not sure I do. Explain."

He was deliberately being dense to aggravate her. Trying to outsmart him, Bailey took the bait. "You do not fondle a woman's behind or breasts in public. Is that clear enough?" She stood stock-still while he regarded her breasts thoughtfully.

"You don't gawk at them, either!" she added, when he seemed disinclined to speak or alter the direction of his gaze.

"What about . . . ?" He lowered his attention to the juncture between her legs.

"Not there, either!"

"Well, you didn't mention it."

Bailey squeezed her eyes closed and began counting aloud, backward from one hundred. She'd gotten to ninety-seven, when she heard the creak of wood and knew Steele was moving toward her. She popped open her eyes.

He chuckled. "Tell me, do you always fly off the handle this easily, or is it just when you're sexually frustrated?"

Bailey snatched the scissors and pointed at the chair. "Sit," she commanded, "and, if you value your eyesight, don't say another word."

THE NEXT MORNING, Steele hid in the back seat of Bailey's old station wagon, while she drove to the shopping center west of Laughlin's Casino Drive. Once there, she parked between a green van and a blue truck to hide him from view when he climbed from the car. He'd call a taxi to take him to the Riverside Hotel and Casino, go to his room, change clothes and check out. Bailey planned to watch from the casino to see if anyone followed him.

"For the last time, will you please go ahead to the airport and wait for me in the baggage area?" Steele asked, sitting up and renewing their second argument of the previous evening. "These men aren't playing games."

"No one will recognize me in my wig," Bailey countered. "If I see anyone leave the casino behind you, I'll pass you and pull into a busy gas station. You stop, too, and I'll slip you a note so you know who to watch for."

"I don't want you to be seen anywhere near me before I'm disguised."

"Tough!" Bailey swung around in her seat. "If you don't know who's following you, how can you be sure you won't lead him to me in the baggage area? Passing you a note in a crowd is safer."

"I'll make sure I'm not followed before I change clothes."

"You can't be positive. My way is best. Now, get out of the car before we attract attention."

Steele exhaled explosively. "Damn, you're a stubborn woman." Bailey smiled. He leaned forward and kissed her cheek.

"Be careful," he warned.

"You, too."

BAILEY ARRIVED at the hotel well before Steele. Stopping at a change vendor, she bought several rolls of quarters and sat down at a slot machine with a view of the registration desk. Despite the early hour, she wasn't alone in the casino, but the jangle of slots rotating was more muffled than it became later in the day. Steele's voice carried easily as he checked out, griping about his losses and the necessity of cutting short his vacation.

Rather than rise and follow him immediately, Bailey fed her machine more quarters. She fixed her gaze on the spinning symbols, but barely saw them, her peripheral vision on the alert for anyone following Steele.

A stocky, swarthy man left one of the slots on her right. He made a short call on the hotel telephone, then headed toward the doors. At the same time, the spinning dials in front of her clicked to a stop in rapid succession. Horns blared. Red lights flashed. Quarters clattered into the money tray.

Bailey froze. Who would walk away from a jackpot? She couldn't follow the man, couldn't leave the machine. She'd attract attention.

Trying to look happy instead of horrified, she grabbed a discarded change cup, scooped up the quarters and rushed to the cashier. Longing to run, but forcing herself to set a casual pace, she left the casino fifty dollars richer and ten minutes behind Steele.

She'd parked in the aisle near the sporty red Mustang he'd rented, but his space was empty. Why hadn't he waited to pull out until he saw her, like he was supposed to? He could've stalled for time by pretending to check the oil or running the air conditioner to cool the car.

Had the man who followed him from the hotel abducted him?

With shaking hands she tried to unlock her car, but dropped her keys. Bending to retrieve them, she heard voices and ducked down instinctively.

"You took long enough! He's already pulled out!"

"So what? We got a tracer on the car. We'll find him fast enough." Car doors opened. Bailey peered over the hood of her station wagon to catch a glimpse of the men climbing into a brown sedan. One was the swarthy man from the casino; the other was sandy-haired. She snapped a mental picture, imprinting their images on her mind and memorizing their license plate number.

Steele's all right, she told her trembling nerves as the men drove from the lot. Scrambling into her car, she jammed the keys in the ignition, then hesitated. She needed to write down the men's descriptions, yet hated to let them get too far from sight.

Clammy with indecision, she wiped her hands on her skirt. She knew Steele's route to Phoenix. Although she might risk a speeding ticket, she could find him. Drawing a deep breath to steady her hands, she pulled pen and paper from her purse and wrote quickly.

She caught up with the brown sedan at Union Pass heading east on Arizona Route 68. Secure in the knowledge they could track Steele with their tracer, the two men traveled at a leisurely pace. Although eager to pass them, she obeyed her common sense warning her not to draw attention to herself by tailgating them.

On the four-lane interstate out of Kingman, she swung around them and overtook Steele. Flashing her lights, she cut in front of him at the exit for the southeastern route to Phoenix. He blew his horn. Glancing in her rearview mirror, she saw him roll down his window and shake his fist at her.

She smiled, certain now he'd follow her when she pulled into a gas station, if for no other reason than to scowl at her for reckless driving. The one in Wikieup wasn't busy enough for her to pass him a note inconspicuously, though. She pressed on to the larger town of Wickenburg and pulled into a combination convenience store and gas station on the main street.

She'd already begun pumping gas when she saw Steele pass by, followed by the brown sedan. Muttering furiously, she insulted his intelligence, yanked the gas nozzle from the tank and slammed it back on the pump. In line to pay for her gas, she had to bite her tongue to keep from telling the man ahead of her to try looking at a map when he asked the attendant for directions to Sun City.

As soon as she pulled back onto the heavily traveled street, a red light delayed her further. Fuming, she decided Steele was deliberately trying to lose her. Why else hadn't he stopped? Or waited in the parking garage as they'd planned?

Unconsciously speeding in her angry rush, she gained on the brown sedan fast. Slowing, she reconsidered her options. She knew which airline terminal Steele was using, while the men had to follow him to the rental car agency. She could go on ahead, park and get a jump ahead of them—and Steele.

Waiting behind the tinted glass of the terminal as Steele exited the rental agency's courtesy van, she saw the brown car stop behind it. The swarthy man got out to follow Steele, then the driver pulled away from the curb and headed for the parking garage.

Steele didn't appear to notice. He entered the terminal and headed for the ticket counter. Mercifully short, the line moved quickly. With his ticket in hand, Steele strode toward the gates. The swarthy man's head swiveled, but his partner didn't appear. He had to follow Steele alone. Pleased by the diminished odds, Bailey trotted after the thug, then almost bumped into him, when he suddenly did an about-face at the head of the corridor to the gates.

Unable to follow him without giving herself away, she rounded the corner, observing that Steele passed through the X-ray and metal detector machines. Stopping at a screen listing arrivals and departures, she glanced back at the lobby area. The sandy-haired man had caught up with his partner, who reached inside his jacket and passed him something, then headed back to the gateway.

Bailey's mouth went dry. He'd had a gun! That was why he couldn't follow Steele through the scanning equipment. He no longer had it, she reminded her thrumming nerves and followed him to the checkpoint.

"Only ticketed passengers may pass through," the security guard informed Steele's pursuer.

"But I'm meeting my husband," Bailey interrupted the man's argument in a nasal voice. The official might've been inclined to make an exception for one, but she figured two would make him less lenient.

"Sorry," the portly guard turned to her, "you'll have to wait here."

She turned to the swarthy man for sympathy. "Isn't this aggravating?" she whined. "They sure can inconvenience us, but can they catch a criminal? Why, just the other day, I told my neighbor, Joan, I said, it's not safe for a woman to—"

"I ain't got the time, lady." The man scowled and pushed past her, back to the lobby where his partner waited.

"How rude!" Bailey hid her smile of triumph with an indignant expression and turned back to the security guard, who looked at her with a pained politeness.

"Please, step out of the way, ma'am," he said.

Bailey crossed to the opposite wall and darted a quick look toward the lobby. The dark-haired man had taken a seat facing the corridor. She didn't see the other man. Had he gone to buy a ticket to get past the guard? Turning back to the gates, she scanned a crowd of people coming toward her and willed Steele to hurry.

She didn't know what he'd be wearing other than sunglasses and his red wig, but she recognized him instantly. Not only did he stand a head higher than those around him, the contained energy of his walk gave him away. "Surprise!" she screeched and launched herself at him the second he cleared the checkpoint.

"What . . . ?" he asked, frowning at her.

"Just kiss me, you dope," she whispered fiercely.

6

STEELE DROPPED his carry-on suitcase, hauled Bailey into his arms and kissed her. Thoroughly. He didn't know what the hell was going on, but he wasn't about to turn down such a welcome invitation. Her arms around his neck, her breasts flattened against his chest, Bailey melted against him.

He caressed her back, his hands sliding easily over the slippery silk of the sleeveless shell beneath her linen jacket. Her lips parted beneath his. Before he could deepen the kiss, though, someone bumped into them, and a chuckled, "Sorry!" reminded him where they were.

He dropped his hands to the wide belt spanning her narrow waist, then settled them on the curve of her hips beneath her long jacket and raised his head. His fogged sunglasses blurred his vision. He lifted a hand to remove them.

"No!" she protested. "Leave them on. We're being watched. You can't let him see your black eye."

Stiffening, Steele pretended to adjust the sunglasses. "Where is he? What does he look like? What the hell are you doing here?"

"There's two of them. One's sitting in the lobby, facing us. He's got on a yellow, knit sports shirt, jeans and a tan, windbreaker-type jacket. Dark and stocky. I think the other one went to buy a ticket so he could follow you through the checkpoint."

Steele's glasses cleared. Glancing toward the lobby, he picked up his suitcase. "I know that one." He kept his voice low. "Does the other one have light hair?"

Bailey nodded.

"They're two of the ones who jumped me. I hope the third is in the hospital." Anxious to get her out of their vicinity, he dropped his free arm over her shoulders and headed up the corridor. Why the hell hadn't she listened to him and waited in the baggage area?

"They have guns," Bailey whispered.

"How do you know that?" He scowled and stopped in his tracks.

"Smile!" she urged. "I'll tell you, later. The crowd is thinning. We can't afford to be singled out." She wrapped an arm around his waist and pressed him to move forward.

"I told Mattie to stay away from your barbells," she added shrilly. He winced and hurriedly resumed their walk toward the lobby. "But he never listens to me. You're going to have to talk to him as soon as we get home."

"What a voice," Steele muttered, realizing she was putting on an act for the benefit of their watcher. "A good spanking may be in order," he said loudly, then ducked his head and whispered, "For you, too. You were supposed to wait in the baggage area."

She shot him a just-try-it glance rather than risk a retort; they were passing the dark-haired man. "That's why I decided to meet you," she whined. "I'm fit to be tied! The boy just goes wild when you're not home." She kept up a loud litany of complaints until they were safely through the lobby to the ticket area, where they passed his partner. Obviously in a hurry to return to the gates, he didn't spare them a glance. When they reached the escalator to the baggage area, Steele glanced behind them and saw no sign of either man.

Bailey looked at him happily. "We lost them!"

He didn't smile back. "You have some explaining to do."

Once they'd reached the solitude of her car, though, Bailey grabbed the offensive. "Why didn't you wait for me in the parking lot in Laughlin?" she demanded, turning the key in the ignition and flipping on the air-conditioning. "And why didn't you follow me into the gas station in Wickenburg?"

"Why didn't you go to the baggage area and wait like you were supposed to?" Steele yanked at the tie he'd donned in the airport, rolled down his window, shrugged out of his sports jacket and ripped off his wig. The heat in the closed car was stifling, the currents blasting from the air conditioner as hot as an oven set on broil.

"Put that back on!"

He ignored her protest. "Look, if you don't listen to me, I can't be responsible for your safety. You risked yourself needlessly. I can't have that. I have to work *alone!*"

Bailey turned to him. "You were deliberately trying to lose me?"

"For your own good."

The expression on her face shifted from surprise to disbelief to anger in rapid succession. "If we're not going to work together, I don't need you," she finally said and indicated his door with a wave of her hand. "You can get out . . . *now.*"

Steele stared at her. The blond wig and heavier makeup altered her appearance, but she was as strong willed as ever. He sighed disgustedly and ran a hand through his matted hair. He could learn how to play blackjack from a book, but he had to admit that Bailey could teach him the subtle intricacies he'd need to carry off his impersonation of a high roller. He sighed again. "Get this car moving so we can cool off, and tell me what happened from the beginning."

"Are we working together?"

"Yes, dammit!"

"Put your wig back on. Those guys could be parked around here."

Steele obeyed sullenly.

After they left the garage and paid the attendant, she began her story. When she said she'd seen one man pass what she thought was a gun to the other, yet still approached the one trying to get through the checkpoint, he exploded.

"You walked right up to him? Face-to-face?"

"He might have talked his way around the guard," she retorted, brushing off his question without glancing away from the heavy traffic. "We'll need to use different disguises when we're ready to check into the Sunburst, though. You should change your body language, too. If I recognized your walk right away, Lana could. You need to shuffle or slouch or something."

Steele barely heard her. "I knew anyone following me wouldn't have a ticket and couldn't pass through the passenger checkpoint. Haven't you heard of hijackings? The guard wouldn't have made an exception."

"That's not always true. I've been to Sky Harbor often enough to know the airlines don't always restrict the gates to ticketed passengers."

"That's not the point!" Her stubborn refusal to see how unnecessarily she'd risked herself infuriated him. He launched into a tirade intending to make her listen to him in the future. "You're a woman," he concluded, "and can't defend yourself like I can. Physically, you're weaker than I am. Remember that and trust me to take care of myself. Act like a woman instead of a fool and don't come charging to my rescue!"

Bailey didn't say another word until she pulled into the lot at the Scottsdale Hotel, parked the car and handed him the keys. "I'll go check in. You can meet me inside with the suitcases, since I'm *much* too weak to carry one." She slammed the door behind her.

Steele counted to ten, then exited and locked the car. He wasn't surprised to discover Bailey had a royal temper; most strong-minded people did. What he'd like to know, though, was how long it would last. Convinced he was in the right, he'd be damned if he'd apologize.

"I'll meet you in the lobby in twenty minutes," she said when they were in the elevator, her gaze fixed on the closed doors. "We can grab a quick lunch before our appointment with the optometrist for our contact lenses . . . if that meets with your approval?" She flicked an angry glance in his direction, then returned to her study of the elevator doors.

"Fine." Steele stared at her profile and groped for words to assuage her temper. "Bailey, I'm just trying to look out for you. . . ."

"I could say the same thing, but a man is invincible, isn't he?" The elevator stopped, and she stepped out, again leaving him with the suitcases.

"Shall I set your bag inside for you?" he asked when they reached her door. Since they'd be shopping, she hadn't packed much and could've carried it easily, but he figured he'd go along with her and ride out the storm.

"That won't be necessary. I can manage." She took the suitcase and slammed the door in his face.

BAILEY TOSSED the suitcase on the bed and opened it, her movements jerky with anger. Steele thought acting like a woman meant obeying his every edict? Cowering in the corner while he took all the risks? She might not have his muscles, but she had a brain. What if the men had been able to follow him through the passenger checkpoint to the gates? What if he couldn't have eluded them long enough to disguise himself? He should be thanking her for her quick thinking instead of yelling at her!

She shook out the black, floral print outfit she'd bought for "Carla" to wear while they shopped and rehearsed their roles, then hung it up and eyed it grimly. The short, tight skirt and matching strapless bustier were provocative, to say the least, especially when combined with her spike heels. Guessing what Steele's reaction to it would be, she'd felt uncomfortable about wearing it when she packed it.

Not now, though. Now she was going to take great satisfaction in flaunting herself, then bidding him a chaste good-night when their shopping spree was over. He clearly expected to call the shots in *her* plan, and she wouldn't be at all surprised if he thought to cut her out of it entirely.

He'd pay dearly for calling her a fool. He wanted her to act like a helpless woman? That was what he was going to get. She'd play the dizzy, blond bombshell to the hilt until he begged for mercy.

Deliberately, she kept him waiting in the lobby for an extra ten minutes. When she appeared, the click of her high heels against the stone floor drew his attention. He rose from his seat on the cushioned, bleached wood couch and removed his sunglasses. His stunned gaze worked up the long expanse of her legs to her short, formfitting skirt and bustier.

"Did I keep you waiting, *Matt*, honey?" she cooed in Carla's Marilyn Monroe voice and wrapped herself around his arm. She emphasized his name because he hadn't worn his wig, although she'd told him they should rehearse their roles while they shopped. He could ignore her plans, apparently, but she couldn't ignore his.

He swallowed, but failed to answer while he dragged his attention away from her cleavage.

Revenge felt very sweet. She lifted her free hand to stroke his cheek. "You know how we women have to fuss to look good for our men."

The look in Steele's eyes said he knew what she was up to, while his grin assured her he'd rise to the occasion. "You're definitely worth the wait, darlin'," he drawled in his deep, Texas twang. "Does this mean I'm forgiven?"

"What do you think?" She slid her hand into the open collar of his shirt and skimmed her fingernails along his neck.

He dropped his hands to her hips and pulled her hard up against him. "Two can play this game, Bailey," he growled. "Be careful. I could throw you over my shoulder and haul you upstairs to my room."

"The name's Carla," she corrected in her breathy voice, "and I'm afraid we don't have time for that. We'd better skip lunch, too, and head straight to the optometrist's." She stepped back, but kept her arm hooked through his and tugged him toward the door.

"You do have the keys?" she asked when they reached the car and she halted at the passenger side. He opened

the door in answer. She got in and reached over to unlock the driver's door, then hurriedly scooted back to her
side.

He slid behind the steering wheel and started the engine, then turned to examine her. Bailey tossed her head,
crossed her legs and faced him. "Like what you see?"

"Very much." He grinned. "How long is this shopping
going to take?"

"All day," she assured him. "I'm very hard to please."
She turned her head to stare out the window. Looking at
him reminded her of his kiss at the airport. Despite the
gravity of the situation, she'd responded to him—and not
only out of relief. She couldn't lie to herself. The feel of
his muscular body against hers, his scent, his taste, even
the angle of his head when his lips met hers—all were
becoming familiar and increasingly intoxicating. Could
her anger continue to numb her body's response to his?

It had to, for her plan to punish him to work.

BAILEY DEFINITELY could hold a grudge, Steele learned.
She didn't just get mad; she got even. The visit to the optometrist wasn't too bad, though. Other than reducing
the white-haired man to a case of blushing, tongue-tied
lust more characteristic of a pimply-faced teenager, she
behaved herself.

Lunch was worse. He didn't think she had to lean quite
so far over the table when she spoke or take such a sensual enjoyment of her mushroom quiche and spinach
salad.

Once they reached Metrocenter, the largest shopping
center in Phoenix, however, she really turned up the
heat. She clung to his arm while they walked from store
to store and rubbed against him at every opportunity.

The clothes she chose to try on hugged and plunged in all the right places—and she modeled far more than she bought. Under the guise of asking his opinion, she shamelessly preened and strutted in front of mirrors.

"What do you think, honey?" she'd ask in her breathy voice, presenting her flawless figure to him for examination. Aware she was taking savage delight in torturing him, he struggled against his body's response.

And lost the battle. His answers grew increasingly monosyllabic. His fingers twitched with the urge to drag her back to their hotel and rip every stitch of clothing off her.

He breathed a sigh of relief when, at last, she decided she'd bought enough for herself and they entered a men's store.

"I'm not sure that's big enough," she said when he came out of the dressing room wearing a western-cut suit.

"It's fine," he assured her. To nix her idea of trying to make him look fat, he argued that a rich Texan could afford a good tailor.

She stepped in front of him, giving him a nice three-way view of her back in the store mirrors. She adjusted his bolo tie, slid her hands across his shoulders and down his arms to check the length of the sleeves. "Yes, I guess it's all right," she agreed. Her torture session, Steele realized, was far from over.

"What about the shirt?" She slipped her hands inside the jacket and ran her hands down his sides, then dipped her fingers inside his waistband. "Not too tight?" She closed the small, remaining distance between them and brought her hands together behind his back.

Then, she made the mistake of smiling up at him.

"That does it," Steele swore and caught her head in his right hand, while his left held her in place. Her lips parted in surprise. Ruthlessly taking advantage of the slight opening, he plundered her mouth with a steaming kiss of hot, frustrated desire.

Her tongue met his, stroke for stroke, and her fingers curled into his waistband, pressing their hips together. Steele grasped her shoulders, stroked her bare, satiny flesh, then shoved himself back, away from her. His chest heaved as he gulped for air and struggled to restrain the passion roaring through his veins and ears. He'd expected her to stiffen, struggle, turn her head, bite him or clamp her lips together—not for a minute had he expected her wild response.

She hadn't been acting. A sensual haziness clouded her light eyes, her breasts rose and fell with the quick, short pants of her ragged breathing, a faint flush pinkened her cheeks. Her lips were swollen and reddened without a trace of lipstick.

The salesman coughed discreetly. "Does that mean you like the suit?" he asked, grinning broadly. Steele couldn't have answered if his life depended on it; he couldn't take his eyes off Bailey.

She blinked, lifted a hand to smooth her wig, swallowed and turned to the man. "I do apologize," she purred with an arch glance at Steele. "Matt can be such a *bad* boy. Of course, we'll take it. Do you carry any Stetsons or cowboy boots?"

She pulled her lipstick from her purse and turned to the mirror. Steele watched her hand while she applied the tube of color to her lips and grinned with satisfaction when he detected a slight tremor. She was a good actress, but she wasn't as untouched as she pretended.

She also kept more distance between them while he tried on other clothes she selected. "Where should we go to dinner?" he asked when she piled their purchases in his arms and led the way to the car.

"It's been a long day, I think I'll just order room service."

"Okay." He unlocked and opened the car door for her.

"Alone."

"What's the matter?" he drawled after he'd settled behind the steering wheel. "Was that kiss more than you bargained for?"

"Shopping exhausts me," she answered evasively. "Shouldn't we get going? It has to be over a hundred degrees."

He started the car and turned on the air-conditioning, but didn't back out of their parking space.

"Which isn't nearly as hot as that kiss. What's the matter? Afraid to go out to dinner with me?"

"Of course not." She stared out the windshield. "I'm tired. It's been a long day."

"Then you won't mind if I join you. I hate to eat alone. We'll order room service, kick back and watch television." He put the car in gear and headed back to the hotel.

ALONE IN HER ROOM, Bailey stripped off her wig and brushed out her hair with hard, angry strokes. She'd made a major tactical error when she'd allowed herself to return Steele's kiss. She'd guessed he wanted to get back at her for tormenting him and hadn't wanted to back down. But the depth of her unrestrained response scared her. No matter how much she didn't want to become involved, her attraction to Steele kept growing.

How was she going to keep him at arm's length while they had a private dinner in her room? And watched television?

Ha! Television was the last thing on Steele's mind.

She tossed the brush aside and paced beside the queen-size bed. To suddenly insist they go to a restaurant would be tantamount to admitting she didn't trust herself alone with him. Steele wasn't above trying a little seduction, but he wouldn't force her. Of that, she was sure.

What she wasn't sure of, though, was her capacity to resist him. Her pacing took her near the window. She glanced out and caught sight of the pool.

That was it! She snapped her fingers. She'd invite Steele to go for a swim, then suggest they order dinner on the patio. Quickly moving to the telephone, she called his room.

"I thought you were tired," he objected.

"There's a hot tub, too. You don't know what walking in spike heels does to your feet and legs."

"I could massage them for you."

"I'll be by the pool if you care to join me." She hung up quickly and pulled her yellow bikini from her suitcase. Minutes later, a knock sounded on her door.

"Erickson massage service," Steele called.

"I didn't order any!"

"Compliments of the hotel," he insisted.

"Thanks, but no thanks." She tied the strings of the bikini bottom over her hips, then slipped into the bra.

"I called downstairs, the hot tub's not working."

"Liar. I can see it from my window." She'd neglected to pack a beach cover so she grabbed a towel and wrapped it around her waist. "Meet you downstairs!"

When she opened the door, Steele stood waiting. "Hi, Bailey," he said, eyeing her black hair. "Nice to see you again."

"Too bad I can't say the same." Like her, he wore a towel around his waist. Averting her eyes from his bare chest, she hurried down the hall to the elevator and jabbed the button, willing it to arrive and end their privacy. "You chose not to wear your wig," she added, her gaze directed straight in front of her. "You can ignore me when I tell you to wear it, but I'm supposed to say, 'yes, master,' and go wait in the baggage area when two hoodlums are after you."

"Still mad, eh?"

He poked her in the ribs. To get a laugh out of her, she supposed. She glared at him, instead.

The elevator arrived. Naturally, it was empty. Fuming, Bailey stepped into it and stabbed the button for the bottom floor.

"Can't we just kiss and make up?" Steele asked, standing so close beside her, their arms brushed.

"Not a chance." Bailey edged away and watched the floor numbers light up as they descended. When they reached the ground floor, she stalked through the lobby to the pool, tossed her towel and room key on a chaise lounge by the hot tub, then crossed to the deep end of the pool and dove into the water.

No one else was around on this weekday evening. Steele easily kept abreast of her while she swam laps. He was healing quickly, but she hoped his ribs still hurt when he lifted his arms above his head to match her strokes. The flesh beneath his eye was still blackened, but the swelling had disappeared and the bruises on his ribs and stomach were fading into yellow.

Not speaking to him, she stopped after her tenth lap, climbed from the pool and stalked to the empty hot tub. She closed her eyes rather than look at Steele when he sat down in front of the jet next to hers.

"What's it going to take, Bailey?" he asked.

"For what?" She opened her eyes.

"To get you to laugh with me again. I miss you."

"That's not all you want."

He grinned, not denying her implication. "It's a start."

His charm wrapped around her, seductive, yet curiously honest. "Promise you won't try and leave me behind again. Admit I didn't take an unnecessary risk today. Consider me an equal partner. Remember I'm not like Carla with nothing to offer besides my body."

"The body is one and the same, and right now Carla has a certain appeal," Steele muttered irritably and shifted closer.

Bailey laughed, but dodged the arm he tried to slide around her shoulders. Steele grabbed her waist, tickling her with his fingers. She squirmed and flailed at his shoulders, but couldn't escape his grasp.

"Quit trying to distract me!" she demanded.

He dunked her in response. When he let her up, he mercilessly attacked her ticklish sides until she could only gasp for air between bouts of laughter.

"Say uncle!" he demanded.

"Never!" Her strength was no match for his, but she knew one way to make him stop.

Sliding her arms around his neck and wrapping her legs around his waist, she kissed him. His hands stilled, his tongue plunged into her mouth and found hers. The sound of roiling water thundered in her ears, mixing with the hammering of her heart as she surrendered to her desire for him.

His hands moved again. No longer tickling, his fingers massaged her outer thighs, edging upward to trace the high-cut legs of her bikini bottom, the curve of her hips and waist, then rising to the sides of her breasts. Cupping their softness, his thumbs slid between their bodies, rubbing the taut nipples straining at the wet, clinging jersey of her bikini.

"Say you'll go upstairs with me," Steele demanded, barely lifting his lips from hers, "or I'll take you right here and now." He slid his hands to the tie holding her bikini bra together.

Slowly opening her eyes, Bailey saw the desire and entreaty reflected in his blue eyes . . . and nodded. Without giving herself time to think or question her decision, she stood. She wanted Steele as much as he wanted her. Neither their pasts nor their futures mattered.

This moment and this night would be theirs.

She stood and reached for a towel. "Better wear this around your waist," she said, grinning and glancing at the bulge in his wet swimming trunks as he rose out of the water.

"You're not exactly unaffected either," he retorted with an eloquent glance at her breasts.

"Just the cold air," she told him lightly.

He grabbed the towel and swatted her behind with it.

When she'd wrapped her towel over her breasts and under her arms, Steele shook his head. "I like to look," he protested, tugging down the terry cloth. The protection of the towel had softened the peaks of her breasts, but the heat of his gaze stiffened them immediately.

Bailey caught her breath. "Then we should get upstairs so you can get a closer look," she said huskily.

"Absolutely." Steele snatched their room keys, grasped her arm and strode toward the lobby.

STEELE CURSED beneath his breath when they had to share the elevator with a middle-aged couple. He wanted to kiss Bailey again, kiss her senseless before she had time to think.

With a nod to the couple, he punched the button for Bailey's and his floor and moved behind the strangers. The button they'd pushed was above theirs. Silently urging the elevator to hurry, he slipped his arm around Bailey and his hand beneath the strap across her back.

Her eyes widened, and she shook her head in silent protest. He grinned and slid his hand down her back, beneath both the towel at her waist and the fabric of her bikini bottom to cup her damp, rounded flesh.

"Steele...!" she whispered, her gaze flying to the backs of the other couple.

He kissed the tip of her nose. The second the elevator doors opened on their floor, he grabbed her hand and sprinted down the hall.

Entering his room, he pushed Bailey to the bed. "We're still wet," she protested, laughing as she landed and he fell across her. "Maybe we should dry off first."

"I can't wait another moment." Steele lowered his lips to hers, silencing any further conversation.

RETURNING STEELE'S kiss with all her pent-up passion, Bailey didn't remember why she'd been mad at him, or why she'd ever resisted his advances. She stretched her length against the hard expanse of his, felt the strings of her bikini slip away and reveled in the feel of flesh against flesh.

She heard Steele whisper, "Let me look at you," but she wouldn't release him, didn't want the delightful friction to cease.

He rolled over and sat her up, cupping her breasts in his hands. She arched her back and raised her arms, lifting her hair from her shoulders, posing for him, glorying in his desire and the feel of his hands stroking her. The long afternoon of pretending indifference while she tried to drive him wild had tortured her as much as him.

He dropped his hands to her waist and grasped her hips, initiating a seductive rhythm. She let her arms fall back to his thighs, reveling in the hard warmth pressing at the juncture between her legs.

When she could bear no more, she curled her fingers into the waistband of his skimpy swimming trunks and slid back, taking them with her and dropping them to the floor when she stood.

Before she could climb back on the bed, he sat up and reached for her hands. "Let me look," he murmured in a raspy voice, holding her arms out from her sides and admiring her nude body. Then his lips traced the path his gaze had drawn. He suckled at each breast, nibbled his way down her flat stomach and lower still. When her knees buckled, he drew her down on the bed beside him, one hand delving into her nest of black curls and the other roaming from one sensitive nipple to the other.

Writhing with pleasure, she tried to pull him atop her, begging him to grant her the fulfillment she craved.

"Not yet," he whispered, easily resisting the pressure she exerted on his shoulders.

"Yes," Bailey insisted. Catching him by surprise, she reversed their positions. "My turn," she explained, bending to plant kisses all over his body.

"Enough," Steele declared suddenly and pulled away from her to reach into the nightstand.

Bailey smiled and slid the sheath on him. From the moment she'd met him, her instincts had told her to trust him. She couldn't have been more right about him, she decided. Then coherent thought fled.

Steele rolled her on her back and entered her.

He moved with exquisite gentleness at first, allowing her body to adjust to their union. Drawing back, he plunged within her again . . . and yet again . . . gradually deepening each thrust. She wrapped her legs around his hips, matching his rhythm, then silently urging him to take her faster, harder.

Their locked bodies strained together, their murmurs mingling and melding into moans, their senses soaring, hearts thundering, until, at last, they shuddered, together, at the summit of pure sensation.

7

BAILEY CLUNG TO Steele when he rolled on his side, pulled her against his chest and whispered soft endearments in a steady stream. She smiled, cuddled even closer and pressed her lips against the hollow of his throat. She felt safe and warm, oblivious to the world beyond his arms. If only she could stop time . . .

"No regrets?" Steele asked, a note of anxiety in his voice.

"Uh-uh." She dragged the husky denial from deep in her throat and stretched against him sensuously. He chuckled and skimmed his hand along her back. "Although I'd meant to drive you insane with desire today, not both of us," she added, propping her head on one hand so she could see his face.

"You did a good job, by the way."

"You inspired me."

They grinned at one another, then kissed and didn't speak again until much later, when hunger drove them to study the room service menu.

"I'd better try Kevin again," Steele said after he'd placed their order and been told they'd have a half-hour wait. "I missed him when I called earlier. Forrest took him out riding today."

"I'll clean up," Bailey said, thinking she'd give him privacy, but he pulled her back when she tried to rise.

"Not without me to scrub your back, you won't." He kissed her, then reached for the telephone again.

Remembering his exuberance the last time he talked to Kevin, Bailey lay back against the pillows, an expectant smile on her lips.

After he dialed, Steele dropped his arm around her shoulders and leaned back next to her. She sat close enough to recognize that a male voice answered the phone, but she couldn't comprehend the words.

"Enjoying your vacation at my expense?" Steele asked in lieu of a greeting. The man at the end of the line didn't laugh. He spoke hurriedly. Steele launched into a string of curses, then cut himself short and listened.

Tense, Bailey strained to hear more clearly, but couldn't.

"Right," Steele agreed. "Nine o'clock sharp." He hung up and leapt from the bed. "Forrest thinks the ranch is being watched." He snatched a pair of jeans from his suitcase and jammed his legs into them. "Dammit!" He paced a few steps, then swiveled back to her. "They must be watching all my friends. How else could they have found him?"

"Kevin's all right?" Bailey asked, more concerned about the boy than how he'd been located.

Steele nodded. "I couldn't stay on the phone to talk to him, though. If Forrest is right, the line might be tapped, and they could trace the number to us here. We arranged a backup plan before we left Connecticut, so all we had to do was pick a time."

He resumed his pacing. "Tom, my friend who owns the ranch, has a plane. He'll file a flight plan for Los Angeles, then radio his intention to stop in Phoenix en route.

By the time he shows up in L.A. alone, we'll be far away from the airport."

He shook his head. "These guys are more powerful than I thought. If they've got enough men to stake out my friends, they're capable of anything."

He sat down on the bed and took her hands in his. "After we pick them up tomorrow, I want you to take Kevin and hole up in a motel until this is over. Forrest can check into the Sunburst with me. I'm sure he knows how to play blackjack. He can be the serious gambler. I'll just be out for a good time."

"No." Bailey pulled her hands from his. "I have a stake in this and want to be there. Besides, two men would be more suspicious than a man and a woman."

"Bailey, please!"

"What if the guys after Kevin found us? How am I supposed to protect him? I am, as you pointed out, no more than a defenseless woman!"

"I'll hire bodyguards, find you a safe place to stay." He paused, reaching out to finger a long, curling strand of her hair. "Don't you see? I need to protect you, just as I need to protect my son."

Bailey batted his hand away. "I'm an adult, your son isn't. I won't be put in the same category." She slid from the bed, away from him. Grabbing one of their towels, she wrapped it around her, high under her arms. "You're also forgetting these men may have murdered my son, husband and brother-in-law. I have a score to settle. I'm *not* going to sit around and play nursemaid!"

Steele stood and opened his mouth to speak, but she rushed on. "If Forrest goes with you, he'll have to concentrate on his playing. He won't be able to study the game to see if it's rigged. You don't know enough about gambling to see it. Even if you did, you can't exactly lean over his shoulder like Lady Luck—unless you pretend to be lovers."

She raked a telling glance over his body. He'd zipped his fly, but had secured neither button nor belt. The fabric gapped at his waist. Not all gay men were effeminate, she knew, but she couldn't imagine Steele passing as anything but the heterosexual male he was.

"I don't think your acting ability can stretch that far."

Steele grinned, but she plowed on, holding onto her anger to fight a flush of desire. "And, if you're not sure they're cheating, how can you report them to the police? No one's going to walk up to you and say, 'I killed Cliff Richards, or I threatened Steele Erickson's son!' You need me there. Forrest can guard Kevin at my house. No one knows I found you. The last place anyone would look for Kevin is across the river from Laughlin."

Steele stalked around the bed to stand in front of her. Bailey lifted her chin and met his gaze evenly, silently telling him nothing he could say would change her mind.

"Once any of us steps foot into a helicopter and goes to that club in the mountains," Steele argued, not heeding her silent message, "he or she will be at these people's mercy. If something goes wrong, Forrest and I would have a chance to fight it out. If you're with me, they could use you against me. Don't you see?" His voice cracked.

Touched by the tenderness in his blue eyes, Bailey stroked his stubbled cheek. "If I go, there's less of a chance anything will go wrong," she said gently. "I appreciate your concern, I really do, but I'm also sure my plan is the best one. No one would expect you to bring a woman. We'll get on the helicopter, gamble for a few days, come back and notify the police. In and out, no problems."

Steele turned his head to kiss her hand. "You can't be sure of that."

"More sure than if you go with Forrest. Doesn't Lana know him?"

He nodded reluctantly.

"That would double the chance of her recognizing you. Even if she's not involved in this, she could give you away by accident."

"I'd rather risk that than you."

Bailey lowered her hand. "The choice isn't yours to make."

Temper flared in Steele's blue eyes. "How can you say that?" He grasped her shoulders and shook her gently, but firmly. "We made love to one another. We didn't just have some fantastic sex! I care about you and want time to explore those feelings, time to let them develop. I think that gives me some voice in this decision. If something happens to you, we won't have a chance for a future!"

Wrenching herself from his grasp, Bailey snatched her room key and headed for the door. "You can *never* count on a future, Steele. I was safe at home when Cliff's truck went off the road. Do you think that gives me any consolation?"

She'd reached the door, but so had Steele. With one hand splayed against it and his arm stiffened, he held it closed.

"They won't kill *me*, though. They can't get my money if I'm dead."

Bailey turned to him slowly. Leaning against the door, she looked at him. "Once you've seen their club, you could expose them. They'd never let you out alive."

Steele raised his other hand to the door and pinned her to it by framing her body with both arms. Bending his head, he kissed her, touching her only with his lips, as if communicating without words.

His kiss was sweet with tenderness, but Bailey only had sadness to return. She never should've made love with him. Such intimacy implied hope for a future, a future she couldn't consider until she'd made peace with the past.

She *had* to go to that club with Steele, *had* to see what Cliff had seen. If the club proved to be legitimate, she'd accept her husband's and son's death as accidental. If not, she'd see the murderers brought to justice.

"You win," Steele said, lifting his head. "We'll do it your way." He grasped the ends of the towel tucked above her breasts. "Now let's go back to bed."

She covered his hands with hers. "No."

Steele frowned surprise but, before he could argue, a knock at the door made them jump.

"Room service," a man called. Bailey dashed into the bathroom. When the waiter left, she came out dressed in one of Steele's shirts.

"I preferred the towel," he muttered, escorting her to the round table by the window and pulling out a chair for her.

Bailey smiled, but didn't respond. She sat and rolled up the sleeves so she could eat. "What time do you want to leave in the morning?" she asked, while he uncorked the half bottle of cabernet sauvignon he'd ordered to go with their steaks.

"Eight o'clock, in case we hit rush-hour traffic. I want to get Kevin away from the airport—fast."

Bailey cut into her filet mignon.

"A toast, first," Steele objected, pouring the wine, then sitting down and lifting his glass.

Reluctantly Bailey lifted the goblet of ruby-red wine and clinked her glass against his.

"To us," he said.

"To success," she countered and sipped the wine. Steele drank, too, then lowered his glass and studied her. Bailey busied herself with her steak.

"Why won't you toast us?"

Bailey set down her fork. "Because there can't be an us until this is over."

His lips tightened; his steady gaze demanded an explanation.

"I told you on the boat. Neither of us is free of our pasts."

"I broke free of my past when I divorced Lana. And you were free enough of yours less than an hour ago." He shot a glance at the rumpled bed.

"That was a mistake."

"That was many things, beginning with wonderful and surpassing extraordinary, but it was *not* a mistake."

"You took it to mean I was prepared to consider a future. I've lived a day at a time ever since Travis..." Blinking rapidly and unable to continue, Bailey reached for her wine and sipped it. "Ever since I lost my future," she amended.

"You lost one future," Steele said softly, "and I regret that, but you can have another."

Refusing to answer, she dropped her gaze to her plate and began to eat. The filet was tender and flavorful, she was sure, but she chewed mechanically. All she wanted to do was finish the meal and escape to the solitude of her own room. She didn't touch her baked potato, asparagus or Bernaise sauce.

Steele ate silently too, but when Bailey returned her plate to the room service cart, he laid down his fork. Ignoring him, Bailey gathered the pieces of her bikini from the bed, her room key from the dresser and headed for the door.

"You're going out in the hall dressed like that?"

"It's only next door. I'll check and make sure no one's around first."

"I can't persuade you to stay?"

Bailey grasped the knob and shook her head without turning.

"I never figured you for a coward."

Bailey stiffened, wanting to deny his accusation, yet unable to deny its truth. She *was* afraid, afraid of the feelings he stirred within her and where they might lead. Her view of the door blurring, she turned the knob, glanced up and down the hall and left.

A LITTLE REPLICA of Steele with blond hair, blue eyes and a sturdy body, Kevin barreled down the steps of the plane and leapt into his father's arms. "Wow! Where'd you get that shiner?" he asked, ripping off Steele's sunglasses. "Did you beat him up? Is he hurted real bad?" Scrambling down from Steele's grasp, he curled his hands into fists and jabbed the air as though fighting an invisible adversary. His sound effects, however, were very audible. "Pow! Bam!"

"Whoa!" Steele planted a restraining hand on his son's shoulder. "Nothing so dramatic. I walked into a door."

Kevin froze in mid-jab and gaped at his father. "Geez, Dad! How'd you do something stupid like that?"

Steele winced and mumbled something about stumbling in a dark and unfamiliar hotel room, then beckoned Bailey to come forward. He introduced her to Kevin and the two men carrying an Airedale terrier in a cage down the airplane's steps.

"Nice to meet ya," Kevin recited by rote, clearly more interested in releasing his dog than meeting her. Leaving Steele to help his son, the two men took more interest.

An attractive man with black hair and hazel eyes, Forrest Hamilton was almost as tall as Steele with a lean, athletic build. The pilot and rancher, Tom Elliot, was short and burly.

Tom couldn't linger but he invited her to visit his isolated New Mexico ranch. His wife, Sue, always welcomed feminine companionship, he explained.

"That goes for me too," Forrest added.

Steele gave him a sharp glance.

"A little competition never hurt anybody," Forrest retorted, grinning at Steele and sliding an arm around Bailey's shoulders.

"Back off, Hamilton," he warned, not responding to his friend's humor.

"Or what?" Forrest glanced at the dog pulling on the leash Steele had tied to the cage. "You'll sic Darby on me?"

"Or I won't introduce you to Bailey's twin sister."

"Identical?" At Steele's nod, Forrest released Bailey and rubbed his hands together in satisfaction. "One for each of us? Sounds great!"

Bailey rolled her eyes and stepped forward to pet the dog. "This sun makes the pavement pretty hot," she told Kevin, "and could hurt her paws. Shall I walk her over to the grass while your dad loads up the car?"

"I'll do it," the boy said, untying the leash, but Steele grabbed it and handed it to Bailey.

"Darby's still stronger than you," he explained. "Let Bailey handle her. She has a dog, too. He's a German shepherd named Max." He turned to Bailey. "Do you think they'll get along?"

She nodded. "Males and females don't fight."

"Unlike humans, eh?" he asked in an undertone.

"Darby listens to me," Kevin insisted. "I want to walk her!"

"You can walk with Darby, but Bailey holds the leash," Steele said sternly, handing it to her. Kevin stuck out his lower lip in a pout, but tagged along with Bailey.

"Darby seems pretty attached to you," she commented.

"I've had her since she was a puppy," he informed her, cheering up enough to brag about how good she was. Bailey kept her attention on the dog.

Kevin looked nothing like Travis, but the sight of his soft, smooth skin, rounded cheeks, small hands and feet and short, sturdy legs stabbed her with memories: Travis looking at her with his big, brown, trusting eyes, Travis slipping his hand in hers when they crossed a street, Travis giggling and stumbling while he ran after Max down the yard . . .

Travis's stricken face when Cliff had tried to tell him he couldn't come along on that ill-fated camping trip.

Had Cliff suspected he might be followed? Had he wanted to be alone with Ron to discuss what he should do about what he'd seen at the casino? Or had he simply thought the extra day would make the trip too long for a four-year-old?

Regardless of Cliff's reasoning, if she hadn't insisted he keep his promise to take Travis, their son would be alive and only a few short months younger than six-year-old Kevin.

As if sensing her inattention, the boy beside her talked louder and louder until his voice seemed to spin and echo inside her head and she wanted to turn on him and scream, "Shut up!"

"I think your dad's ready for us," she said instead, and hurried toward her station wagon.

"Do you mind if I drive?" Steele asked, when they joined him. "I'm afraid we've pretty well filled up the back with Kevin's toys and luggage. We'll be more comfortable if you sit between Forrest and me."

"Let Kevin sit up front," Bailey suggested. "He won't take as much space or block your view in the rearview mirror. I'll keep Darby company in the back seat."

"You don't have to do that," Steele objected.

"I want to." Bailey opened the back door, ushered the dog onto the seat and sat down beside her. Kevin scrambled onto the front seat.

"The mens should sit together," he announced.

"Men," Steele corrected with an annoyed glance at Bailey, then slid behind the steering wheel. Forrest climbed in next to Kevin, seat belts were fastened and Steele drove off. Bailey leaned her head back and closed her eyes, blocking out the sight of Steele's profile and his fond smiles while Kevin prattled about his adventures on the New Mexico ranch.

Darby inched her head into her lap. Bailey rubbed her ears and struggled to tune out the sound of Kevin's high-pitched voice. Life wasn't fair, she reminded herself. She shouldn't begrudge Steele his son because she'd lost hers. Yet she couldn't help herself.

She was right to end their relationship before it went any further. If they were to have a future, he'd expect her to accept his son as her own. She couldn't do it. She could barely stand being in his vicinity.

When they reached her home, she masked her feelings with a smile and told the men to store all but Kevin's favorite toys in the garage. Leading Darby to the backyard, she made a mental note to pick up Max from Bonnie's as soon as the men finished unloading the car. Sooner or later, her sister would discover her houseguests, but she preferred later.

Unlocking the kitchen door, she headed for Travis's room, not even aware she was doing so until she stood in the doorway. She gasped at the sight of Kevin rummaging through the chest of toys.

"Whose room is this?" he asked, standing and moving to the lower bunk. He sat down and picked up the worn rabbit perched on the pillow.

Don't scream, Bailey ordered herself, her gaze fixed on Kevin's hands carelessly twirling the stuffed animal by its ears. Her heart thundered in her ears.

"Must be a baby to sleep with this old thing."

Unable to speak, Bailey crossed the room, plucked the rabbit from his grasp and set it out of reach on a closet shelf. Drawing a deep breath, she turned back to Kevin.

"It was my son's. He died when he was two years younger than you. If you intend to sleep in this room, you will treat everything in it with respect." Aware she was shaking, she sank down at the opposite end of the bed.

Kevin regarded her in silence for a few moments. "Do you miss him?"

Surprised by his solemn question, Bailey answered honestly. "Very much."

He nodded. "My granddaddy died, I miss him, too. He was a boxer. He had funny teeth that would come out, like this." He stuck his lower jaw out and pulled his lips back. "Only he could turn them upside down."

False teeth, Bailey realized and smiled. Touched by his ability to relate her son's death to his own loss, she blinked several times to clear her vision.

"Daddy says he's happy in heaven with my grandma. She died when Daddy was a little boy like me." Clasping his hands together in his lap, he swung his legs back and forth and looked around the room, then stood and climbed on a chair to see the pictures on the shelves. "Is this him?" He touched the glass of a framed photograph, but she didn't reprimand him.

"Yes. His name was Travis."

"And who's this?" He touched her wedding picture.

"My husband, Cliff. He and Travis died in a car accident." She swallowed. "They're happy in heaven together, too."

"You live all by yourself?" He climbed from the chair and stood in front of her.

Bailey nodded, but didn't speak.

"I live with my Dad. I have a mom, but he says she's sick and that's why she doesn't live with us or visit me. She sends me presents sometimes, though."

"Maybe she'll get better."

Kevin shook his head. "Dad doesn't think so."

Bailey didn't know what to say. "I bet he's real happy to have you to live with," she said, shifting to a happier subject.

"Yeah." Obviously dismissing this topic, Kevin wandered around the room, looking to her for permission before touching anything. It didn't hurt as much to say yes, she discovered, as it would've when she first walked into the room.

When he returned to the toys, she stood. "Do you want the top or bottom bunk?"

"*You're* going to sleep in here, too?" he asked with such undisguised disgust that Bailey laughed.

"Well, your dad has to sleep in my bed because he's too big for one of these," she explained.

Kevin was not appeased. "Dad!" he screamed at the top of his lungs. Steele came running, with Forrest right behind him.

"I don't have to sleep with *her*, do I?" Kevin asked.

Steele looked at Bailey, who nodded firmly. "I can think of a better arrangement," he answered, holding her gaze, "but it's her house."

"Yuck!"

"Wait a few years and you'll change your tune," Forrest told him, grinning broadly. "What about me?"

"You can go to a hotel," Steele growled.

"I have sleeping bags and foam pads," Bailey told Forrest. By putting Kevin in Travis's room and getting Forrest out of the way, Steele probably hoped to seduce her back into his bed. "I'll make you up a comfortable place on the floor in the living room."

"We'll talk about this," Steele said, clapping a firm hand on Forrest's back and ushering him from the room.

"I'll take the bottom bunk, okay?" Kevin said when they were gone. "Darby likes to sleep with me."

Max had slept with Travis, Bailey remembered, but she fought the pain the memory stirred. For a moment she thought she heard Max's excited bark, but Kevin distracted her, asking if he and his dad could use the softball gloves hanging on the wall.

To delay a response, she reached out to finger them and realized how stiff they'd become from lack of use. "Of course," she said with effort. Kevin could grow bored confined to her yard, she reminded herself, and had to be kept occupied. "I have some saddle soap in the garage you can use to soften them up."

Bailey marched out to the garage with Kevin tagging behind. She'd just closed her hand around the round tin of saddle soap when she again heard Max's familiar bark. She groaned; she hadn't imagined the sound earlier. Her sister had arrived. Snatching some clean rags and handing them to Kevin, she sent him into the house, then hurried to the front yard in hopes of sending Bonnie away.

She was too late. The red compact car parked at the curb was empty, and she heard her sister's voice coming from the back deck. Rounding the corner of the house, she saw Forrest and Bonnie smiling at one another, Steele observing their interaction with a look of amusement and Jenny peering at Kevin, who had just emerged from the house. She climbed the steps to the deck. Forrest and Bonnie barely spared her a glance, but Jenny clapped her hands and gurgled, "An-Bay-wee." Bailey swept her into her arms when Max, followed by Darby, dashed onto the deck for a quick hello.

"You didn't mention you were bringing guests back from Phoenix," Bonnie said, the commotion drawing her attention away from Forrest.

"An unexpected change of plans," Bailey answered, pleased this much was true. She hadn't told her sister the true purpose of the trip to Phoenix. Lies seemed to breed more lies. "I suppose you brought Max over because you knew something was up," she changed the subject.

Bonnie nodded.

"Have you met everyone?"

Bonnie nodded again, her gaze straying back to Forrest. "Steele was telling me you have quite a houseful."

"I'm sure he was." Bailey darted a black look at Steele. The man didn't give up. He was still trying to get Forrest out of the way, so he could renew his seduction of her.

"If it would help, I offered to let Forrest use the Hide-A-Bed at my place."

"I'm sure we can manage," Bailey said, her dry tone letting her sister know she had nothing to do with Steele's bright idea.

"I invited Bonnie and Jenny to stay for dinner," Steele said in the ensuing silence. "Shall I help you make the burgers?" On the way home they'd stopped at a grocery store, where Kevin had been allowed to choose the menu.

"That would be nice." Bailey set Jenny down and stalked into the kitchen, barely waiting for Steele to close the door behind him before she launched her attack. "Manipulating Bonnie into offering Forrest a place to stay isn't going to change my decision."

Not responding, Steele crossed the kitchen to the refrigerator, where he'd put the hamburger away.

"I'm not sharing your bed, and I don't want my sister involved in this."

He still didn't answer. He carried the package to the counter and opened it. Washing his hands at the sink, he grabbed a handful of meat and slapped it into a patty.

Eyeing his profile, Bailey pulled a plate from a cabinet and set it on the counter beside him. The lines in his face had deepened with repressed anger, but his voice was mild when he finally answered.

"All I did was introduce Forrest as a friend." He plopped the huge patty on the plate. "She looked like she wanted to ask questions, but Kevin joined us. She was smart enough to guess I didn't want to explain anything in front of him. Forrest started playing with Jenny and got to talking with Bonnie. When he said he'd be sleeping on the floor of your living room, she invited him to her place."

"That does not sound like my cautious sister." Bailey pulled potatoes from a cabinet and dumped them in the sink. Kevin had also requested french fries.

"I didn't suggest it. All I said was we'd be pretty crowded here." Although Steele didn't raise his voice, he slapped the hamburger in his hands for added emphasis. "Since you insist on going through with this, I think it's a good idea for Forrest to stay with her. He can keep an eye on Jenny and her, as well as Kevin, when we check into the Sunburst." He paused.

Bailey nodded her agreement with this reasoning.

"She seems quite taken with him," he added. "Apparently *she's* not afraid to give a man a chance."

Scrubbing the potatoes, Bailey kept her head down rather than respond to his implication that she was afraid. "Tell Forrest to keep his mouth shut, I don't want Bonnie to know what we're planning."

"You haven't told her?"

Bailey shook her head.

"Why?"

"I don't want to worry her."

"She wouldn't approve," Steele guessed. "At least one of you has some sense."

"She still has Jenny!" Bailey turned on him. "You still have Kevin. Easy for the two of you to say, 'go on with your life.' Well, it's not that easy!" She spun away, and Steele took her place at the sink to wash and dry his hands.

"Don't touch me," Bailey said, when she felt his arms wrap around her waist. Steele pulled her back against him, but she held herself rigid.

"Bonnie and I aren't asking you to forget Travis, we're reminding you that you still have a life to live. You can't bury yourself in the past."

Bailey stared at the oak cabinet in front of her. "I want to know why my son and husband died. Is that too much to ask?" She slid from his loose embrace and faced him.

"It is, if you have to risk your life to do it."

"I'm not risking mine anymore than you're risking yours."

Steele shook his head in disagreement, but spoke softly. "I've said I'll do it your way. Why are you still angry with me?"

"You mean why won't I act like a submissive little woman content to warm your bed and stay home with your son?"

"You know I want more than sex from you."

Yes, she did know that. Bailey slammed a cutting board on the counter and yanked open a drawer to grab a knife. With her back to him, she began slicing the potatoes into french fries.

"You're not afraid of dying, you're afraid of living," Steele accused. "Afraid of loving me."

She felt the weight of his gaze boring into her back, but she refused to turn. "You should start the coals. Kevin is probably hungry."

After a moment, she heard the squeak of her pantry opening, the rustle of a bag of charcoal, then Steele's steps and the slam of the kitchen door. Bailey continued slicing the potatoes, but she worked on automatic mode. Her mind repeated Steele's words, "Afraid of living . . . afraid of loving me."

8

BONNIE NOTICED the strained silence between Steele and Bailey during dinner, but Forrest's conversation, with occasional help from Kevin and Jenny, eased the situation and captured her attention. Slightly over six feet tall and well-muscled—if not developed to Steele's body-builder proportions—and with ruggedly handsome features, Forrest had attracted her on a physical level immediately. What captivated her now, though, was the intelligence gleaming in his hazel eyes.

A member of a local theater group, she envied him the Broadway plays he'd seen and understood when he admitted he'd originally moved to New York City from the Connecticut countryside to pursue an acting career.

To support himself between scarce acting jobs, he'd worked as a guard for a security firm, then expanded into investigative cases. "I had to adopt different personas to worm information out of people and found I was good at it." He grinned. "I made more money at it, too, so I opened my own agency."

The gleam in his eyes when she returned his smile told her he reciprocated her interest. He excited her like no other man she'd been dating, and she liked his easy manner with Jenny. She hoped he'd accept her invitation to stay at her home to give her the opportunity to get to know him better. Bailey might call her more cautious nature "chicken" but, in this case, she suspected their positions were reversed.

The simmering tension between Steele and her sister, she sensed, was due to Bailey not following her advice— as usual. Clinging to her grief, her sister wasn't giving Steele a chance.

Bonnie wasn't going to make the same mistake. Forrest could end up being a disappointment, but she was willing to give him the opportunity to prove otherwise.

She was highly curious about his and Kevin's presence in Bullhead City, but his captivating conversation kept her mind off of it until the kids were put to bed. When the four of them adjourned to the back deck, she demanded, "What's going on?"

Intent on receiving an answer, she paid no attention to Forrest when he sat beside her on the glider. Bailey perched on the porch railing, while Steele pulled up a folding chair.

Her twin hemmed and hawed, glanced vainly at Steele for help, then broke down and explained. Clamping her lips together to keep herself from interrupting, Bonnie listened grimly.

"You lied to me!" she exclaimed when Bailey was done. "You told me Steele was going to the police!"

"He is," Bailey mumbled, her eyes downcast, "as soon as we know for sure what's going on at that club." She lifted her gaze. "I didn't want to worry you, you know what a—"

"Don't call me a chicken!" Bonnie jumped to her feet to confront her sister. "We're not talking about courage or cowardice here. We're talking common sense. You can't go to the club, someone may recognize either one or both of you. Use the brains we were born with! Or did I get them all?"

"We'll be well-disguised," Bailey insisted, with a stubborn tilt to her chin Bonnie knew well, "and I'm going, no matter what you say, so save your breath."

Bonnie tried to reason with her anyway, even when Steele told her he'd used the same arguments. Forrest listened closely, but diplomatically withheld an opinion.

"No more keeping me in the dark," Bonnie finally said, dropping back on the glider and crossing her arms beneath her breasts. "If you get an invitation to this club, pass me a message at the registration desk telling me when you're leaving and when you're due back."

"If anything should go wrong, they might come after you," Bailey objected. "I think Forrest should take you, Jenny and Kevin out of town. We've both got vacation time coming. People will think we're traveling together."

Bonnie shook her head, deliberately giving Bailey a taste of her own stubbornness. "Mom and Dad have been wanting to take Jenny to Disneyland and can take Kevin, too." She glanced at Steele, who nodded his approval. "You can tell them you're dating Kevin's father and want a few days alone together."

"I want you out of the way, too," Bailey insisted.

"Tough. My job at the registration desk will give me a perfect place to keep an eye on you. If we know when to expect you back, Forrest can pretend to be a tourist wandering on the roof when the helicopter lands. If you don't get off, we'll call the police."

"We'll be your backup," Forrest addressed Bailey, "unless you let me go. Then the two of you could be Steele's and my backup."

"I'm going." Bailey's tone brooked no more argument.

Now allies against her, Bonnie and Steele exchanged a frustrated glance.

"You'll need identification to support your disguises," Forrest broke the ensuing silence. "Even if you use cash to pay for your room, these guys might do a credit check before they invite you to their club."

"They couldn't have done one on Lana," Steele put in.

"She could've been hired as an entertainer, though," Forrest pointed out, "rather than invited as a gambler."

"How can we fake a credit history?" Bailey worried.

"I'm a private detective," Forrest reminded her. "I've got contacts. I can arrange it."

"Use a pay phone and take a lot of change with you." Steele advised. "Credit card calls can be traced. If you were seen with Kevin on the ranch, they'll be looking for you."

"How did you know the ranch was watched?" Bonnie asked. "How could they have known about it?"

"We noticed a repair truck working on the telephone wires. Tom called the company. They had no record of any unit sent to that location." Forrest shook his head.

"Tom and I competed as teenagers in bodybuilding contests," Steele answered her second question. "He never went professional, but we stayed friends. Lana's been there, she could've told them." He curled his right hand into a fist and punched the open palm of his left. "I thought the ranch was so isolated, Kevin would be safe. They probably checked there first."

"Don't blame yourself," Forrest said. "This is no penny ante organization. They could've staked out everyone you knew."

Bonnie stared at the jagged silhouette of the mountains rising on the other side of the river. Forrest's statement seemed to make the night more sinister, the shadows beneath the trees deeper, and the reflection of the moon on the river, cold and ominous.

Unable to bear the sight and longing for the normalcy of her home, Bonnie stood. Her sister's plan was insane, but Bailey's mind was made up. Further argument was useless.

Forrest rose, too. "Is your offer of a place to stay still open?"

"Sure." Bonnie repressed the grin threatening to split her face. "Why don't you get your suitcase, while I get Jenny?"

Bailey and Steele walked them to her car. Jenny fussed over being strapped in her car seat, but then promptly fell asleep again.

"Mad at me?" Bailey asked.

"Furious," Bonnie agreed without hesitation. "But I'm stuck with you as my twin." She kissed her sister's cheek, then moved to Steele and surprised him by hugging him. "Take care of her," she whispered.

"I'm trying," he answered wryly.

Bonnie drove, although Forrest offered to take the wheel. Alone with him, she suddenly felt awkward, a feeling that intensified when they walked into the privacy of her small town house. What was she doing inviting a strange man to sleep in her home?

"I'll just put Jenny to bed, then make up the Hide-A-Bed for you," she said, heading upstairs. She didn't hurry, though, while she changed Jenny's diaper and laid her in her crib. Since she'd blatantly returned Forrest's interest throughout the evening, would he expect her to join him in bed? While the thought had its attractions, she wasn't ready for such intimacy. When she gave her body, she gave her heart.

Brushing a dark curl from Jenny's cheek, she bent to kiss her. How would her child react to having a man in the house? Forrest had black hair, at least she wouldn't call him Da-Da, like she did blond men. "Call him Mr. Hamilton," she whispered and straightened. She couldn't allow Jenny to get too attached to him. Risking her own heart was dangerous enough. She wouldn't risk her daughter's.

Descending the stairs to the living room with bed linens in her arms, she prayed Forrest wouldn't turn into one of her groping Casanova dates.

He hadn't dimmed the lights, which she took as a good sign. He had pulled out the Hide-A-Bed and stretched out on the mattress while he read her newspaper. "Newsprint rubs off," Bonnie said, dropping the bedclothes and plucking the discarded sections of paper from the arm of her pale blue, chintz-covered couch.

He lowered the newspaper. "The things a bachelor doesn't know." He grinned at her, a lazy, sexy grin that took her breath away.

"It's a new couch," she said lamely, kicking herself for sounding like a housewife. "I never should've bought such a light color, I can't let Jenny near it when she's eating—"

"I understand," Forrest interrupted, peeling his body off the bed and standing next to her. "No need to explain."

She was babbling, Bonnie realized and retreated to the other side of the bed. For all her grand advice to her sister, her attraction to Forrest now unnerved her. The man lived on the other end of the country; how had she thought a relationship could develop from their attraction?

Grabbing a sheet, she snapped it open. Forrest caught one side and, while they worked, kept up a light patter of conversation. He examined her corners, "to see if he'd tucked his in right."

He hadn't and insisted she show him how to make her tight, right-angle folds. "So that's how people get the sheets to stay on the bottom all night," he said in wonder when they'd finished. "I usually wake up with my feet sticking out in the cold air."

"Poor bachelor." Relaxed and laughing, Bonnie teased him. "The government should reinstate the draft so men can learn how to make a bed!"

"You're much nicer to look at than a drill sergeant." His grin faded; his eyes focused on her lips.

Say something, Bonnie commanded her suddenly paralyzed tongue, but all she could do was stare back at him.

Slowly, leaving her time to retreat if she chose, Forrest lifted his hand and caressed her cheek with his knuckles. "I know we've just met but, if I don't get a good-night kiss, I'll never sleep for wondering what it would be like."

Let Bailey be the chicken this time, Bonnie thought and closed the distance between them.

He brushed her lips with his gently, leisurely exploring their contours, then gradually fitting them to his. When the pressure of his mouth on hers increased, Bonnie slipped her arms around his neck, nestling her body to his, and experienced a strange sense of belonging.

While she hadn't made love with any of the men she dated, she'd kissed them, but had felt nothing other than awkwardness. Sensing the men's rising passion, she'd withdrawn, unable to return it.

Passion, too, simmered beneath Forrest's kiss, inciting her own. The kiss remained unhurried, though, ripe with promise, yet complete in itself, not merely a prelude to the satisfaction of desire.

Lifting his head, Forrest said, "I'm glad you're not going to that club."

Entranced by his kiss, Bonnie blinked, not understanding him.

"I wouldn't want to risk losing you when I've only just found you," he explained.

His words pleased her, but the thought of her sister's dangerous plan brought Bonnie back to reality with a thud. She lowered her arms from his neck.

"I'm sorry, now I've made you worry about your sister." Forrest embraced her.

Unresisting, she rested her head on his chest, comforted by the steady beat of his heart.

"Believe me, Steele will do everything in his power to keep her safe. He's in love with her, you know."

"Did he tell you that?" Bonnie raised her head to see his face.

"He didn't have to. He may not realize it, yet, but I knew it the second I got off the plane and saw the way he looked at her."

"I hope you're right, but Bailey won't make it easy for him."

"I noticed." Forrest chuckled. "I'm glad you're the levelheaded twin."

"Do you mean the chicken?" Bonnie asked, suspicious of comparisons with Bailey.

"Not at all. I mean you combine beauty and common sense." He dropped a kiss on the silly grin Bonnie felt forming on her face. "Now go to bed before I forget we just met and try something you wouldn't want me to—yet."

Bonnie arched an eyebrow at his self-confidence, but followed his advice. Did Forrest feel the same indefinable connection to her she did to him? Was love at first sight possible? Or was this an infatuation?

Time would tell. She'd get to know Forrest, but wouldn't turn her life upside down. She'd continue her normal routines—including her social life—as though she didn't have the fascinating Mr. Hamilton living under her roof.

She might've been a bit hasty in inviting him to stay in her home. She found it just as difficult to pick up the pieces of her life as her sister did. At least she'd give Forrest a chance, though, which was more than Bailey seemed to be giving Steele.

She wouldn't be the chicken this time.

AFTER FORREST AND BONNIE left, Bailey bid Steele a cool good-night. Steele let her go without argument. Pushing her to resume their intimate relationship only seemed to make her more stubborn.

In the ensuing days, he bided his time and spent his days with Forrest and Kevin, often taking Bailey's boat down the Colorado River, far from Laughlin. Kevin still thought they were on vacation and, as long as Steele kept him occupied, asked few questions.

After Kevin went to bed at night, Bailey started the blackjack lessons, but Steele couldn't concentrate. The object of the game was simple enough: to get a higher count of cards than the dealer up to, but not over, twenty-one. The problem, however, was remembering strategy. When to say "hit me" or "one more time"—that is, ask for another card—and when to say "I'll stand." This, Bailey explained endlessly, depended on the dealer's faceup card as well as his own hand.

He'd look across the kitchen table at her while she discussed mathematical probabilities and his mind would wander to the few short hours she'd been his. Sensing his lack of attention, she'd threaten to substitute Forrest for his part in the plan.

The thought of Bailey fawning over Forrest in her role as Carla would renew his concentration briefly, but then . . . then she'd touch her wavy hair . . . and he'd remember its scent and silky softness against his face. Othertimes his gaze drifted from the cards on the table to the swell of her breasts . . . and he'd remember how they'd filled his hands, how she'd moaned when he suckled at their stiffened peaks. . . .

Periodically he tried to provoke her in hopes she'd get angry enough to repeat Carla's seductive performance to punish him, but she refused to take the bait. Her pale blue eyes turning into icicles, she'd stab him with a silencing look.

When she came home from work, she didn't even dress in shorts anymore. He'd catch a glimpse of her lovely legs when she walked through the door and into her room, then she'd emerge in loose-fitting cotton slacks and an oversize shirt. Whether she meant to hide her sexuality from him or herself, he wasn't sure, but it didn't help him. He just looked closer and used his memory to fill in the gaps.

When he suggested they work on their tans for their disguises, she refused. "I sunbathe on my lunch hour. In this sun, it doesn't take much." The glance she gave him told him she figured he was searching for an excuse to get her clothes off. He didn't deny it. Her strong will now annoyed rather than impressed him.

She still wanted him, he was sure. He rarely wore more than running shorts and saw her gaze longingly at him when she thought he wasn't looking.

All was fair in love and war. And, in his opinion, their relationship fit both categories. She wouldn't touch him, though, and always moved away if he so much as brushed her arm. Kevin could crawl all over her, and both Darby and Max received ample attention. Steele vehemently hoped her nights were as long and lonely as his.

The closest he got to her was when she decided his hair was long enough to be permed. The proximity of her breasts while she stood by his chair and rolled his hair onto curlers was sheer torture. If they'd been alone, he would've grabbed her, but she'd foreseen such a possibility and enlisted Kevin's giggling assistance to separate and hand her the small squares of tissue paper she wrapped around each lock of hair.

To explain to Kevin why his father was submitting to the perm, she told Kevin that Steele had lost at cards.

"A man never reneges on a bet," Steele added, trying to recover his suffering masculinity.

Kevin still giggled.

FORREST'S ROMANCING of Bonnie wasn't faring much better, Steele learned on one of their boat trips. He'd been sleeping on her couch for two weeks, and she still accepted calls from other men. She had even gone on a date.

"This morning, I told a guy I was her lover and not to call back again," Forrest admitted sheepishly, while they watched Kevin build sand castles on an inlet beach they'd found. "I've about had it. We talk, we kiss, then she says she needs more time. Time for what?" Before Steele could hazard an answer, he continued, "And she tells me not to be so friendly with Jenny. I like the kid! All I have to do is grin at her and she giggles. You should hear her try to say Mr. Hamilton. Bonnie won't even let her say Forrest. I suggested 'uncle,' and she went through the roof."

Steele nodded, finding it easier to understand Bonnie's caution than Bailey's. "Relationships get complicated when you're a single parent," he explained. "You've got to think of someone besides yourself. It's bad enough if things don't work out and you get hurt, but you don't want your child disappointed, too."

"How's Kevin taking to Bailey?"

"He likes her, but he knows we'll be going home one of these days. If Bailey and I don't make it, he'll just remember her as a nice lady." He paused. "I hope."

"And you?"

Steele didn't hesitate. "I'll forever kick myself for letting her get away."

"I know just what you mean."

They sat in silence for long moments.

Abruptly Steele stood. "I'm not letting that happen," he vowed.

Forrest rose with him. "What are you going to do?"

"Confront her. Tonight. The hell with this patience bit. I'm getting nowhere fast and I want this settled before we check into the Sunburst." Not only had his black eye and bruised ribs healed, he had learned from Forrest today their fake credit backgrounds were complete.

Forrest clapped him on the back. "I'll make a move on Bonnie, tonight."

Steele grinned. "Let's shake on it."

STEELE THOUGHT he'd never get Kevin to bed. When at last he closed the door to his son's room, he went to the kitchen and told Bailey their credit references were ready. All they had to do was get her parents and the children off to Disneyland, then they could go to Phoenix, pick up their contact lenses, rent a car and return to Laughlin to check into the Sunburst.

"We still have to dye your hair, as well as mine, and you'll never pass as a high roller unless your blackjack improves," she objected.

Steele hid a grin, pleased she'd reacted according to his plan. "I've got the basics," he maintained, "but I need higher stakes to motivate myself."

"Such as?" She arched an eyebrow suspiciously.

"I've heard of strip poker, how about strip black-jack?" He thought of Forrest guiltily. This strategy wasn't exactly the direct confrontation he had implied he would take.

"Not a chance." She crossed her arms beneath her breasts in what Steele thought was an unconsciously defensive gesture.

"Chicken?" he taunted. "Afraid you won't be able to control yourself in the presence of my naked body?"

"You prance around half-naked already."

Steele grinned. Her irritated tone told him he'd read the longing in her eyes correctly. "I'll start fully dressed."

Bailey regarded him thoughtfully. She couldn't, he knew, resist a challenge and was weakening. "What if Kevin wakes up?"

"He hasn't since he got here, right? I've lived with him for six years. He'd sleep through a nuclear attack."

Bailey swung away from him and closed the curtains over the windows by the kitchen table. Steele went to his room to throw on jeans and a T-shirt, then returned to the kitchen and pulled the cards from the drawer.

"No touching," she stipulated when they sat down in the breakfast nook across from one another. She took the cards and shuffled them.

"Unless invited," Steele qualified.

"In your dreams." She slapped the cards on the table in front of him. "Cut." Steele divided the cards. Bailey picked them up. "Place your bet."

"Your bra," he said promptly.

"You bet your own clothes," she snapped, "not mine."

"My shirt. Your bet?"

"Dealers don't really bet," she objected, obviously having second thoughts on her agreement.

"But they serve as the bank, they take or pay off the bets."

"They don't get to use their own strategy."

"I'll play two hands. One for me and one for you. You undress only if your hand loses."

"You'll lose mine deliberately!"

Steele grinned. "If you don't agree with how I play your cards, your loss won't count."

"Fair enough. I bid a shoe." She ignored his scowl. "Go over rules and strategy."

"Dealer must hit on sixteen or below and stand on seventeen and above." Steele closed his eyes as if reciting in his sleep. "I always hit on a count of eleven or less and stand on seventeen or more."

He paused, drew a deep breath and opened his eyes. "My course of action from twelve to sixteen depends on the dealer's up card and the laws of probability, which means remembering a helluva lot of combinations!"

Bailey smiled. "We're playing for big stakes, tonight, so you'd better sharpen your memory."

"No review?" Steele asked, startled.

"My modesty is at stake, here."

"I have a very good memory. And you have nothing to be modest about." He let his gaze wander over her oversize shirt. "Be a good teacher and go over the combinations again." He sat up straighter on the bench and focused on her face. "I'll pay close attention."

"I bet you will," Bailey muttered, but she rapidly recited the numbers. Steele leaned forward, concentrating hard. Trying to confuse him, he thought, she barely paused before going into her explanations of when to split or not to split pairs and when to double down, or double his bet. He'd studied the notes he'd made on previous evenings, though, and the numbers slipped into place in his mind. He intended, not only to win at blackjack tonight, but to seduce Bailey right out of her clothes and into his arms.

SHE WAS CRAZY TO HAVE agreed to Steele's suggestion, Bailey scolded herself, while she dealt. He obviously had more in mind than learning blackjack. His attention had wandered throughout their previous lessons, and she had a strong suspicion she knew where it strayed. The same thoughts kept her awake at night.

The hardest test of her willpower, though, was when Steele was with his son. The love between them was so palpable she felt as if she could reach out and touch it when they wrestled on the floor or played catch in the yard. Their laughter, Steele's gentleness, Kevin's loud exuberance and the contrast in their sizes pulled at her heart, piercing her with memories of another father and son. Yet, she couldn't look away, couldn't repress a smile at the picture they made.

Kevin was no perfect child; he frequently tested the limits of his father's patience, especially at bedtime. Once the battle was over, though, and Steele held his son in his lap on the couch by the table lamp and read him a story, Bailey had to fight the urge to kiss the two blond heads shining in the light.

She forced her attention back to the game when Steele lifted the corner of his first two cards. He glanced at the dealer's faceup card, a five of clubs, and her heart thumped nervously. Or was it in anticipation? She wasn't sure.

"Hit me," he said. She laid a three of spades next to his two facedown cards.

"One more time." She gave him a five of diamonds.

"I'll stand."

He lifted the edges of the next hand, her hand, and repeated the process. His face revealed nothing.

"This isn't poker," Bailey reminded him, longing for a clue.

He smiled, but only said he'd stand.

Bailey flipped over the dealer's hole card, a king, adding ten to the five already faceup. Praying she'd bust, which would mean both hands Steele played would win, she drew a card. A four gave her nineteen.

Steele flipped over his down cards, adding a two and a four to the three and five, for a total of fourteen. "Guess I lose," he said, feigning his disappointment, she suspected.

He stood and worked his T-shirt out of his jeans. Slowly. Tantalizingly. Bailey tried to wrench her gaze away, but her eyes refused the command. His shirt inched up, revealing the jut of his pelvic bones above his waistband, his flat stomach, the line of his sternum lying like a valley between the rounded mounds of his pectoral muscles.

Bailey stared and remembered. His taste was slightly salty, his scent a blend of soap, spicy after-shave and indefinable male essence, and the texture of his flesh a contrast of smooth satin stretched over iron brawn.

Steele pulled the shirt over his head, tossed it aside and flexed. She sucked in her breath. Ridges of muscles, veins and sinews popped into view, then rippled when he shifted position. She stared and held her breath, afraid it would emerge in short, quick pants of desire.

He turned his back and flexed again. His broad shoulders seemed to widen and his waist to shrink, an exaggerated yet stunning version of the male physique.

Lifting her hand to her mouth, Bailey released the breath she held in a long, silent stream, then drew it in again.

Steele was a dizzying combination of brute strength and gentleness. And she wanted him.

But he wanted too much from her.

"How about a little music?" Steele suggested and left the room.

Bailey reminded herself to breathe, blinked and looked around the kitchen, as if she'd never seen it before, then shook her head to clear it. The sighing strains of B.B. King's guitar and voice drifted into the room, soulful and seductive.

Steele definitely was playing for very high stakes, she realized, stakes that might improve his concentration, but she held serious doubts about her own.

"By the way, I'll take your shoe," Steele said, returning and extending his hand. "Your cards came to seventeen." He flipped them over and sat down.

Bailey handed him her sandal and wished she'd also worn socks.

9

STEELE SPOKE LESS and less as the game progressed, using hand signals to indicate whether or not he wanted another card. Bailey fell silent, too, until the only sounds in the room were the bluesy beat of B.B. King's music and the slap of cards on the table bathed in light from the wicker-shaded globe above it.

Steele's concentration was total; his decisions rapid and wise. He never looked at Bailey until a hand played out but, then, he fixed her with a gaze intense with determination—and a longing that seemed to heat the air and draw the breath from her lungs.

Time, always on the dealer's side, ticked by, stripping them bit by bit of their clothes. Steele's athletic shoes and socks followed his shirt onto the bench by Bailey's side. She relinquished her other shoe, then the ribbon decking her ponytail. When she surrendered the elastic band holding up her hair, Steele blew her a kiss. Her gaze riveted on his lips, soft and moist in the frame of his strawberry-blond beard, and she quivered, her skin prickling as if anticipating the rasp of his beard and the slide of his lips.

He stood to remove his belt, unbuckling it and slowly slipping it off, one loop at a time. Her senses heightened, she could hear the leather rub against the denim of his low-cut jeans, taunting her, tempting her hands to join his and tear the fabric from his body.

She clutched the cards instead, and dealt another hand. If Steele noticed she neither shuffled nor asked him to cut, he didn't comment. The next hand he played for her busted, exceeded twenty-one. Try as she might, she couldn't fault his playing. The strategy she'd taught him was based on probability, not certainty.

She had to relinquish either her slacks or her blouse.

Steele leaned back and crossed his arms over his chest, waiting and smiling in anticipation. Remaining seated, she wiggled out of her slacks and passed them to him over the table.

He still made no sound, but the blue of his eyes darkened, and his grin widened when he accepted them. Again they played, with Steele dressed only in his jeans and briefs and Bailey in her oversize shirt, bra and panties.

They both lost the next round. Steele stood. Bailey glued her gaze to his face. She couldn't block the sight of his hands dropping to his waistband from her peripheral vision, though, or deafen her ears to the slide of his zippered fly.

Escaping her control, her gaze dipped down his magnificent chest and lower still to follow the denim over his hips. His briefs, pale blue against his sun-bronzed skin, were low-cut and snug, revealing the bulge of his masculinity. When he stepped from his jeans, she dragged her attention back to the cards and tried to shuffle them, but they fell from her trembling grasp.

"Your turn," Steele said, still standing.

She fumbled at the buttons on the cuffs of her long sleeves. When she lifted her fingers to the front of her shirt, he sat down, his gaze following the path of her hands as she undid each button.

The music ended when she lowered her head and slid the shirt from her shoulders. She heard his breath catch at the sight of her breasts lifted, yet barely covered, by the sheer, lilac lace of her demi-bra.

"Deal," Steele said, his voice ragged and harsh in the silence.

Bailey lifted her gaze to his and shook her head. "Game's over," she said, her voice barely above a whisper. She rose and stood before him. "You've more than won the right to touch."

He leaned back, his gaze roaming over her breasts, then meandering down her flat stomach to the curve of her waist and hip, then coming to rest on the shadowy triangle beneath the lilac lace at the juncture of her legs.

Heat seemed to follow the trail his eyes blazed. Unclasping the front of her bra, Bailey bared her breasts. He buried his face in her softness, suckling at first one rigid tip, then the other, while his hands slipped her last strip of clothing over her hips and down her legs. Bailey filled her hands with his hair, his shoulders, his back, with every part of him she could reach, granting herself the touch she'd wanted for so long.

Suddenly Steele stood, sat her on the table and snatched his jeans from the bench seat. Jamming his hand into a pocket, he pulled out a foil packet. Bailey took it from him, while he pushed his briefs from his hips. Together, they slid the sheath in place.

Claiming her lips in a searing kiss, Steele gripped her bare bottom, lifted her and entered her in a single thrust. Locking her legs around him, Bailey rocked her hips, flexing and squeezing her inner muscles and rubbing herself against him.

Their breathing quickened; their skin glistened. Sensation spiraled. Suddenly Steele staggered and laid her across the table, scattering cards to the floor. He drove within her, and they hurtled over the brink, beyond control, beyond reason.

When they calmed, Steele straightened his arms and lifted himself to look into her flushed face. "Bailey, I—"

A pounding at the front door interrupted him. "Bailey! Open this door!" Although muffled, the sound of Bonnie's voice was unmistakable.

Steele cursed. Bailey rolled away from him and scrambled for her clothes. "Get dressed," she hissed, then dashed for the bedroom, yelling to her sister to wait a minute. Rather than bother with buttons, Bailey dropped her shirt and slacks on the floor of her closet, yanked a lavender tankdress from a hanger and pulled it over her head, then stumbled into a pair of sandals.

"Bailey, I know you're in there!" Bonnie's shouting and pounding at the door were more audible in the bedroom. "Let me in this minute!"

Bailey ran for the bedroom door and bumped into Steele.

"Slow down," he advised when she bounced off him. "She's not going anywhere. Listen to her, she's going to wake up Kevin, not to mention the whole neighborhood."

Combing her fingers through her hair, she hurried down the hall.

Kevin opened his bedroom door.

"Go back to sleep," she told him, "everything's all right."

"Dad?" Kevin called anyway.

"Coming," Steele answered.

Bailey rushed to the front door.

She almost laughed to see her sister wearing the same lavender dress, but Bonnie's distraught expression sobered her.

"There you are!" Her sister rushed into the living room. "It took you long enough! You've *got* to do something about Forrest Hamilton. He's driving me crazy. I want him out of my house!"

Bailey had barely closed the door when Forrest slammed it open.

"Erickson!" he bellowed, then stopped short at the sight of the twins. "Where the hell is he?"

Dressed in a pair of jogging shorts, Steele joined them. "Keep your voices down," he snapped, "Kevin's trying to sleep."

"Make your friend stop trying to run my life," Bonnie told him, "and I'll be happy to leave."

"You and your great ideas, Erickson," Forrest growled, balling his hands into fists. "I should deck you."

"Don't blame me for your problems," Steele retorted. "*We* were doing just fine until you two busted down the door. You're responsible adults, so get outta here and settle your own problems." He crossed the room and opened the front door.

"Start at the beginning," Bailey said, drawing her sister down to sit on the couch. During their lunches throughout the past two weeks, Bonnie had confessed her growing attraction to Forrest, but wisely, in Bailey's opinion, had decided to take it slow.

Bonnie needed little prompting. "Bad enough he gives the third degree to any man who calls me on the telephone, but tonight, he had the gall to invite himself along on my dinner date with Jim Davis! Greeted Jim at the door and asked if he could join us!"

Bailey thought Steele's cough sounded suspiciously like a choked chuckle, but Forrest claimed her attention. "A desperate man has to take desperate measures," he explained sullenly, dropping into a chair facing the couch.

Bonnie ignored him. "This is after he'd told Jim on the phone this morning he was my live-in lover. Luckily, Jim had enough sense to phone me at work and ask what was going on."

"What did Jim do?" Steele asked. He'd closed the door, but remained stationed beside it, not hiding his eagerness to bid their unexpected guests farewell.

"He said no, of course. We'd barely ordered dinner, though, when the waitress asked if I was Bonnie Hayword and said I had a phone call. Wood-brain over there—" she jerked her head in Forrest's direction "—was on the line, whispering sweet nothings. I hung up and told Jim that Mom had called because Jenny was sleeping over and wanted to say good-night. Then, when the waitress brought our main course, she also delivered a dozen red roses and announced they were from ham-head who wanted me to hurry home!"

Steele didn't disguise his snicker of laughter this time. Bonnie glared at him. Bailey didn't dare look at him for fear she might laugh, too. Jim, she knew, was a nice man, but Bonnie had been seeing him for two months and the relationship was progressing nowhere.

"Next, this violin player waltzed up to our table and played all these lovesick songs, stopping only long enough to say they're from no-mind until Jim gave up and offered to take me home. I suggested going somewhere else, but he figured pea-brain would call all over town until he found us again."

"You didn't use your credit card, did you?" Steele asked Forrest worriedly.

Forrest shook his head. "I took the numbers off a bill I found of Bonnie's."

"What? You embarrassed me, ruined my date, and I'm going to have to pay for it?" Bonnie leapt to her feet and stomped across the carpet to stand over Forrest's chair.

"I'll pay you back." Forrest opened his arms to reach for her. Bonnie hastily retreated. "Now, tell them what happened when you got home," he taunted. "Tell them how you walked into my arms and—"

"You grabbed me!"

"Kissed me," Forrest continued, rising to his feet. Bonnie backed up another step. "Kissed me like there was no tomorrow, like you were drowning and I was a life preserver, kissed me until the damned phone rang and that guy reminded you to be mad at me!"

"What you did was rude! You had no right to interfere with my date!"

"I had every right!" Forrest grabbed for her, but Bonnie rushed back to the couch and, yanking Bailey to her feet, took refuge behind her. "I'm in love with you!"

Bailey gaped at Forrest, feeling totally ridiculous at her position in the middle of his declaration of love. She tried to step aside, but Bonnie moved with her.

Kevin broke the awkward silence. "What's all the yelling about?" he asked, standing in the arched opening to the hallway, rubbing his eyes and squinting against the bright lights.

Forrest hunkered down in front of him. "Sometimes men and women have disagreements and fight," he explained, "when all they really want to do is kiss and make up."

"Yuck!" Kevin dashed back to his room.

Forrest turned to Steele, who nodded, and they moved in unison toward the women. "You're speaking from a strictly male viewpoint," Bonnie said, again swiveling around Bailey.

"And you'd better be sure which twin you grab," Bailey warned, turning in circles with her twin when Steele closed in on them, too.

Both men halted uncertainly.

Bailey grabbed Bonnie's hand and broke for the door. "Got your keys?" she yelled.

"Left 'em in the ignition!"

From the backyard, Darby and Max barked their disappointment at missing the excitement while the sisters ran down the front walk, jumped into opposite sides of Bonnie's car and roared away.

"They didn't even follow us from the house," Bonnie said, glancing in the rearview mirror.

"Is that disappointment I hear in your voice?"

"Surprise," Bonnie retorted. "After what I went through tonight, I wouldn't put it past Forrest to club me over the head and drag me by the hair to his cave."

Bailey couldn't repress a chuckle. "Kind of makes you feel wanted, though, doesn't it?" she asked and, at the answering curve to her sister's lips, burst into full-fledged laughter.

"I'm driving, Bails! Don't make me laugh!"

Bailey couldn't stop, though. "Wood-brain? Ham-head?" she shrieked until Bonnie had to pull over to the curb and join in her laughter.

"They were beautiful roses," she sputtered, "but I had to give them to the waitress so I wouldn't hurt Jim's feelings! And the violinist played all my favorite songs!"

"Sounds pretty romantic to me. How can you be mad at him?"

"Be-because I love him!" Rather than sobering at her confession, Bonnie broke into fresh gales of laughter.

Bailey stared at her. "Bonnie, you're giving true meaning to men's complaint that they don't understand women. *I* don't even understand that one!"

"It's either cry or laugh, and I'm fresh out of tears." Bonnie hiccuped, giggled, shook her head and drove the car back onto the road.

She didn't speak again until she'd parked in her driveway and they'd entered her kitchen. "We're going to need sustenance to carry on this conversation," she said. "Get the butter and eggs from the refrigerator. I'll get the flour, sugar and chips."

Bailey grinned, remembering how chocolate chip cookies had soothed their high-school heartaches. Working together in an unforgotten rhythm, they measured and sifted, creamed and beat, then dropped what batter they didn't eat onto baking sheets. Bonnie slid the cookies into the oven, Bailey set the timer, and they sat down at the round table in the center of the room.

"I want a future with Forrest," Bonnie said without preamble, "not just an affair."

"You should get together with Steele," Bailey mumbled.

"He wants to marry you?" Bonnie sat up straighter in her chair.

Bailey shrugged. "He's making noises about the future, but how can I trust anything beyond the moment?"

"Life's a gamble, just like cards," Bonnie argued. "What happened to us can't stop us from living.

"What about you? If you love Forrest, why are you sitting here with me? Why did you go out with Jim?"

"Because Forrest not only lives in Manhattan, he has his own business there. I have to think about Jenny. I don't want to raise her in a place where I have to worry about gangs, drugs and drive-by shootings."

"Maybe Forrest would move here. How can you tell me to try again, while you're running away from a man you want?"

"I have Jenny to think about," Bonnie said softly, "while you have everything to gain and nothing to lose."

"What's that supposed to mean?" Bailey shoved away from the table and stood.

"You could go to Connecticut with Steele, Bails. I'd miss you and so would Mom and Dad, but none of us would begrudge you another chance at love . . . and another family."

"Oh, right!" Bailey flung her arms up in an exasperated gesture. "Just have another baby, like when you lose a dog and people tell you to run to the pound and pick out a new puppy?"

"You know I don't mean that."

Bailey looked away from the compassion in her sister's face. She did know better. Her nerves and emotions felt as jumbled as the images in a turning kaleidoscope, and she was taking it out on Bonnie. "I'm sorry." She managed a wan smile. "The cookies should be almost done. Let's forget about men and gorge ourselves."

"Milk or coffee?" Bonnie asked.

BAILEY ARRIVED HOME the next morning to find her liquor cabinet empty and Steele and Forrest suffering from the effects of overconsumption. Kevin and the dogs greeted her loudly. The two men nursing coffee at the kitchen table clutched their heads.

"Men should discover the advantage of overindulging in sugar instead of alcohol," Bailey told them cheerfully. Neither she nor Bonnie had made any decisions about their love lives—or lack of them—but she was sure they felt better than either of the two bleary-eyed men.

"What would you like for breakfast?" she asked Kevin.

"French toast!"

"With bacon," Bailey decided, slamming a frying pan onto a burner. "I can smell it, just by thinking about it."

Forrest groaned and let go of his head to clutch his stomach. Steele staggered for the door. "Don't go too far," Bailey called after him. "I want to dye your hair today."

"Is Bonnie going to let me back into her house?" Forrest asked.

"Not until Steele and I check into the Sunburst."

"Do I have a chance with her?"

"Not with you in New York and her here."

Setting the burner on low, Bailey turned to study Forrest's reaction. He frowned and tried to think, then gave up the effort and headed out the door after Steele.

"What's woman trouble?" Kevin asked, moving his toy cars from the floor to the vacated table and taking a seat. When Bailey frowned her puzzlement, he explained. "That's what Daddy said was wrong with Uncle Forrest and him."

Bailey smiled. "I think you'd better ask him, okay?"

Kevin jumped off the bench and sprinted for the door.

"But not right now," she added. "Wait until he feels better."

"I hope I don't get it," he said, dashing back to the table. "I don't like to be sick."

Bailey chuckled and assured him woman trouble wasn't contagious. After they ate, she took mercy on the men and called them inside. "Alcohol is dehydrating," she informed them, "and so is this heat, even if you're in the shade. I made you some juice and toast. Eat, then sleep it off. I've got aspirin, too, if you didn't find it already."

"You're an angel of mercy," Steele said, grabbing his glass of juice. "Does this mean you'll keep me company while I nap?"

"Don't push your luck." Bailey smiled at Steele's disappointed expression. "I'll take Kevin out while you recuperate."

"Will you call Bonnie and tell her I'm dying?" Forrest asked, reaching for the stack of toast. "And my last thoughts are of her?"

"Sure." Bailey turned to Kevin. "Want to meet my parents? My dad plays a kazoo better than anybody. I bet he can teach you."

"Can Darby come?"

"She has to stay out in the yard with Max."

"Don't let him bring back a kazoo," Steele begged.

BAILEY'S PARENTS READILY agreed to her idea of taking Kevin as well as Jenny on a trip to Disneyland, although they were disappointed she hadn't introduced them to Steele.

"We're taking things slowly," Bailey explained, when her mother caught her alone. "If I bring a man in this house, Dad will do his interrogation routine, and I'll never see him again."

She didn't like lying to her parents anymore than she had to her sister, but figured lying was better than endangering or worrying them. She assuaged her conscience by promising herself to tell them the truth when everything was over.

Much to Steele's dismay, Kevin returned home with a kazoo. Both men were feeling better, but Steele still ordered his son outside with the noisy instrument. When Bailey produced the dye for his hair, he kicked out Forrest, too.

The instant they were alone, Steele pulled her into his arms for a deep, lingering kiss. Their breathing was ragged by the time he lifted his head. "I . . ." he began, but Bailey pressed her hand against his lips.

"Don't," she begged, afraid of what he might say, "don't say a word, please."

"Why?"

Bailey lowered her head to his chest and listened to the thumping of his heart. *Because,* she silently answered, *I can only take one day at a time.* He deserved so much more, but that was all she had to give.

"Because I don't want to argue," she said, lifting her face to his. "Mom and Dad are willing to take the kids to Disneyland in the morning. I made reservations for us at the Sunburst for tomorrow night. We'll talk when this is over."

"Promise?" Steele asked, searching her face. She nodded, then quickly changed the subject.

"Forrest can drive us to Phoenix early tomorrow. We'll rent a car, pick up our contact lenses and drive back to Laughlin. I'm going to Bonnie's again tonight, so she can help me do my hair. Any questions?"

"Will you come home and sleep with me?"

Bailey shook her head. "Tomorrow will be a long day. We'll need our rest," she explained.

He frowned, then suddenly brightened. "Only one room at the Sunburst, right?"

"Of course, but you'll have to keep your mind on your gambling."

"Yeah, but look how much better I do with the right motivation!"

"I'll see what I can do," Bailey promised. She reached up to cuff him on the cheek, but found herself stroking his soft beard, instead. "Now, go take a shower and wash your hair so I can dye it."

"I'll make it a cold shower." Steele kissed her again. "Until tomorrow night."

10

"ARE YOU SURE YOU WANT to do this?" Bonnie asked her sister. "It will take years for your hair to return to its natural color."

"Our hair's so dark," Bailey explained, setting bottles on Bonnie's bathroom vanity, "the only way to change the color is to bleach it, then dye it. As you and Steele keep pointing out, this plan is dangerous. I can't risk a wig." She pointed to a bottle. "Start with that one." She bent over the sink.

Applying the chemical to her sister's hair, Bonnie resisted the urge to again try to dissuade her from accompanying Steele. It was useless, and she didn't want to argue on what could conceivably be their last evening together.

"Will you dye it back when this is over?" she asked, clinging to a positive outlook.

"As close to the original color as I can get." Bailey's voice was muffled by the towel she held over her face. "You don't think I'm going to let people tell us apart at this late date, do you? Especially at your wedding."

"You mean your wedding," Bonnie corrected. "You and Steele will be sharing a room, remember. I imagine he can be pretty persuasive." She wrapped a towel around her sister's head.

"To put it delicately," Bailey agreed, straightening and waggling her eyebrows meaningfully. "I'm taking one day at a time, though. How about you? With Jenny and Kevin in Disneyland, I don't think Forrest will want to shake hands and watch television."

"We're going to talk," Bonnie said firmly. "I plan to sit him down and explain how love, to me, means working toward a future together. I'm not a footloose and fancy-free single woman. I have Jenny to consider. I want to know how he feels about marriage and children. If he's throwing around the word 'love' just to get me in his bed, he can forget it."

"Are you going to remember this little speech when he touches you?" Bailey's light eyes twinkled.

Bonnie colored; she could feel the heat rise in her cheeks. Trust her sister to zero in on the weak spot in her plan. "I'm not letting him touch me until we talk."

"Right." Bailey grinned.

"Take Max and Darby out back," Bailey directed Kevin when he arrived with Forrest and Steele at Bonnie's town house the next morning. "Straight through the kitchen." She held the front door open for the two men striding up the pebbled walkway. Bonnie hovered behind her, holding Jenny in her arms as if her daughter were a breastplate protecting her heart. Conspicuously missing was her bravado of the previous evening.

"Did something go wrong with your hair?" Steele asked, eyeing the scarf Bailey had tied around her head to cover her new hair color.

"Just being extra cautious," she explained. "I could be recognized since we're traveling in my car." She lifted her face to accept his kiss.

Their teeth ground together because Forrest caught sight of Bonnie and shouldered them aside in his haste to reach her. He plucked Jenny from her grasp, thrust the child at Steele and hauled Bonnie into his arms.

Bonnie never said a word.

Jenny latched onto Steele's beard and pulled.

Before Bailey could loosen her niece's surprisingly strong grip, Kevin returned. His yell of "Dad!" caught Steele's attention, if not the kissing couple's.

He jerked his head around, leaving several strands of beard in Jenny's hand. Bailey grabbed her, while Steele groaned and rubbed his face.

"Uncle Forrest's gonna get sick with woman trouble again!"

"No, he isn't," Steele assured him, repressing a grin and looking at Bailey. "You only get woman trouble when they're *not* kissing you."

"Huh?"

"Never mind. You'll understand when you're older."

"I'm *never* gonna kiss no girl!" His hands on his hips, Kevin glared at his father.

Chuckling, Steele hunkered down in front of him. "How about a goodbye hug and a kiss for your dad?"

Squinching his small features in a frown, Kevin studied Steele's altered appearance and considered the request. "I won't lose no bet to no girl, neither," he declared. "You look funny!"

"Yeah, but you love me, anyway, right?" Steele opened his arms.

"I guess." Despite his qualified answer, Kevin hugged and kissed his father, then promised to behave at Disneyland.

Grinning from ear to ear, Forrest and Bonnie joined them. In the flurry of leave-taking, Kevin looked perilously close to tears. Steele again hugged him.

As they drove away in the car, Steele muttered, "I should be the one taking him to Disneyland instead of chasing after Lana."

"He'll have a great time with Mom and Dad." Bailey reached for his hand and squeezed it. "After the next few days, you'll be free to take him anywhere."

"If nothing goes wrong."

"Nothing will. We'll make a good team." She leaned over and kissed his cheek. "You worry too much."

Knowing it was a lost cause, Steele resisted the impulse to again try to persuade her to allow Forrest to take her place in their scheme. Unable to share her confidence, he fell into an uneasy silence.

Bailey was quiet, too, while they picked up their rented luxury sedan, said goodbye to Forrest and drove to the optical firm to pick up their extended-wear contact lenses.

When Steele stopped in a bathroom to study this final touch to his disguise, he had to admit Bailey had planned well. His eyes were now hazel-green. The color of his curled hair was a shade darker than strawberry blond, yet lighter than a carroty orange, and looked as natural as his beard. With his beige Stetson, pale blue western shirt, crisp denims and cowboy boots, he almost didn't recognize himself—and was sure Lana wouldn't. His leather belt, with the name Matt scrolled into the leather, was a distinctively western touch, Bailey had told him. Tipping his hat at his reflection, he headed to the waiting room to meet Bailey.

If he hadn't had such a vivid recollection of the orange, formfitting, ribbed cotton knit sheath she'd worn that morning, he would've walked right past her—although not without a second glance.

She'd removed her scarf. Her hair was now a tawny brown streaked with blonde, blending naturally with the cocoa brown of her contacts and deepening her tan. Her flashy hair and jewelry, boldly colored dress, matching manicure and pedicure, and gold, high-heeled sandals perfected her disguise as a woman who devoted her time to her appearance and to pleasing men—if their wallets were thick enough.

To demonstrate his appreciation of her transformation, Steele examined her from head to foot when she rose from her chair and sashayed up to him. "Looking good, Carla, honey," he drawled in his Texan accent.

"You, too, big boy," she cooed, draping herself over his arm and leading him to the front desk to pay for their lenses.

Once alone in the car and on the road to Laughlin, she explained how she'd had to "double-process" her hair. His dye would wash out in six to eight weeks, while her long hair would take years to return to its natural hue. Steele realized with relief that she was taking their plan very seriously.

Dismissing his concern for her sacrifice, she grilled him on their fictional pasts while the miles flew by. "Don't drop your Texas drawl even when we're alone," she advised, "and don't even think of me as Bailey. Something could startle you into an unthinking reaction. We can't afford a single slipup. Remember to slouch a little, too. Body language is a dead giveaway."

Then she launched into a review of blackjack strategy. Steele answered easily, and gradually they fell silent. When they topped the hill overlooking Bullhead City and the casino-crowded stretch of the Colorado River, Steele pulled to the side of the road. "I want you to know something before we arrive," he said, unfastening his seat belt and turning to face Bailey. "I've been fighting you coming along on this because I thought you'd be a handicap. No." He pressed a finger against her lips to silence her indignant protest. "Let me finish." She subsided.

"After my mother died, I practically grew up in my father's gym and, back then, gyms were pretty exclusively male. Muscle made the man, and women were weak, gentle creatures who needed to be protected."

Bailey harrumphed her disagreement.

"My experience with Lana reinforced that opinion." Steele turned to stare out the windshield at Laughlin, unable to stop the bitter twist of his lips. "Not only did she lack the strength to fight her compulsion, she wouldn't even admit she had a problem. Then I met you."

He swung back to Bailey, took her hand and kissed it. "I knew you were a strong-willed woman from the moment you insisted on dragging me off the beach, but I still . . ." his voice trailed away, and his gaze slid away from her face " . . . still wished you'd stay behind this morning."

"And now?" Suspicion tinged Bailey's voice.

"Now I realize how well you've planned this whole thing, how your brains might get us out of a scrape better than my brawn." Needing to hold her, he reached over and unfastened her seat belt.

Half laughing and half crying at the same time, Bailey met him halfway. When he lifted his lips from hers, she reminded him, "I told you we'd make a good team."

"A team for the rest of our lives," Steele pledged. "I love you and, when this is all over, I want to marry you."

He tried to hold her gaze with the force of his own, but she dropped her long, dark lashes over her eyes and stared at a point below his chin.

"Can't we talk about this later?"

"No." He felt rather than heard her sigh, then she pulled free from the circle of his arms.

"That day on the beach, when I touched you, something came alive inside of me," she confessed, raising her gaze to his. "Kind of like Sleeping Beauty, who woke up when the handsome prince kissed her." She smiled, and Steele smiled back with hope and encouragement.

"I didn't think I'd ever feel anything again. I didn't want to." She paused, searching for words. Steele pressed his lips together, forcing himself to give her time.

"I love you," she finally said. Steele reached for her, but she flattened her hand against his chest and held him back. "But I can only give you a day at a time. I'm not ready to make promises for the future and don't think you are, either."

"What the hell do you mean by that?" Disappointment made him speak sharply.

She winced, but her gaze didn't falter. "I need to know, for sure, what happened to Cliff before I can let his memory go. And you need to see Lana again."

Steele shook his head vehemently. "Those are excuses, Bailey," he snapped. "You're still fighting your feelings! Fighting me! I can understand the hold your past has on you, but don't assume I'm in the same position. If Kevin hadn't been threatened, I wouldn't give a damn about Lana."

"Your feelings for her are so strong, Steele, don't you see? Look at yourself in the mirror, look at the emotion on your face whenever her name comes up!" Her voice cracked, and she swallowed heavily.

"It's hate, Bailey! Hate for what she's done. Because of her, Kevin's in danger. How can you think I'd forgive her for that?"

"I have to wait and see."

Steele exhaled, as if he could expel his anger through sheer force of will. "Let's get this the hell over with, then," he growled, sliding back beneath the steering wheel. Glancing at the road behind him, he pressed the accelerator so hard, the tires spun on the gravel when he pulled out.

Bailey had admitted she loved him, he reminded himself, while he drove down the mountain toward Laughlin. Marriage was the next logical step. What he needed to do was get her to the privacy of their hotel room, where their feelings could speak for themselves. Then he could lead her to trust in their future.

PARKING IN THE circular driveway leading to the main entrance of the Sunburst Hotel and Casino, Steele jumped from the car and flipped the keys to the doorman. "Bags are in the trunk," he said, crossing around the car to open Bailey's door.

She flashed a long expanse of leg before accepting his hand. The orange-jacketed attendants gawked at her and almost tripped over their feet as they dashed forward to take their bags and park the car.

Pulling his money clip from his pocket, Steele flaunted a thick roll of cash and handed out five- and ten-dollar bills as if they were pennies. "I'm feeling lucky tonight, boys," he boomed. "Let the dealers know, Matt Logan can hear the cards a'callin' his name."

He splayed the fingers of one hand against the small of Bailey's back and followed the bellboy carrying their suitcases through the orange-and-yellow carpeted arcade. Inside the swinging doors, cool air fanned his skin; muted lighting and a glittering decor greeted his eyes; and the cacophony of jangling slot machines filled his ears with the false promise of easy money.

"Buy me some silver dollars, honey," Bailey begged prettily in her breathy voice when they passed a giant slot machine.

"Later, baby," Steele drawled, smiling indulgently, but increasing his pressure on the small of her back to hurry her toward the registration desk—and the privacy of their room. He felt her stiffen slightly when they reached the desk and guessed she recognized the clerk.

Her face betrayed not a hint of nervousness, though. She fixed the leering man with a bored smile while Steele completed the registration form. "Send a bottle of champagne up," Steele said, accepting their room key, a computerized card. "Your best. And whatever you have in the way of fruit and cheeses. We'll have a bite to eat and, ah, unwind from our trip before we hit the tables." His wink at the clerk told the man what kind of unwinding he meant.

THEIR ROOM WAS ONE of the most expensive in the hotel, on a corner with a view of the river and boasting a wet bar as well as a king-size bed. Bailey hid a smile when Steele cut short the bellboy's explanation of the room's features, hurriedly tipped him and ushered him from the room. The desire in his eyes stirred her own.

"Tell me you love me," he demanded, advancing on her, "and don't give me any if's, and's or but's." She stared at the determined set to his features in surprise and dismay, then swallowed nervously. Waiting for her answer, he settled his hands on her hips and slowly gathered the fabric of her dress with his fingers, working it up her legs while he nudged her toward the bed.

"I told you how I felt," she said evasively, but retreated willingly. The back of her knees hit the bed.

"I want more than that." He pushed her no farther.

"You're asking for more than I can give!" She spoke in an agonized whisper, torn between love and fear. She'd only begun to live for the moment, how could he demand a tomorrow?

"Not if you trust your feelings," he insisted, "like I trust mine. I love you, nothing's going to change that. Believe me." His fingers continued to caress her hips in lazy circles, inching her dress higher and exposing her bare thighs. The coolness of the air-conditioned room wrapped around her legs, heightening her desire for Steele's warm caress.

Grasping the lapels of his western-cut shirt, she yanked open the snaps and slid her hands up the smooth expanse of his chest and over his wide shoulders, then tugged at his neck to bring his lips down to hers.

"Say the words," he demanded again, refusing to bend. "Three little words and not one more." His fingers had reached the hem of her skirt, and he raised it to her waist. Then he pulled her hips forward, brushing the hardness of his groin against the softness of hers, yet denying her the full thrust of his erection.

Bailey moaned, wanting him, needing him, loving him. She tried to press herself harder against him, but his hands on her hips held her in place.

"Say it, Bailey."

"I love you!" she cried, unable to fight him or her feelings any longer. "Damn you!"

Laughing, he pivoted and dropped onto the bed, pulling her down on top of him. He claimed her lips in a long, deep kiss—until he tasted the warm salt of her tears.

She hid her face in the crook of his shoulder.

"What is it? Did I hurt you?"

She shook her head and drew a deep, shuddering breath, then lifted her face to his. "When you break down a dam, you have to expect some flooding," she pointed out, smiling through her tears.

Touched, Steele gently kissed her wet cheeks. "I love you," he murmured.

Bailey's smile turned into a sly grin, and she wiggled against him suggestively. "Maybe you'd better prove that."

Her dress and Steele's shirt lay in a crumpled pile on the floor by the time a knock announced room service. Bailey slid between the sheets and pulled them up to her neck, but she needn't have bothered. Steele shielded her from view with his body when he answered the door, grabbed the items he'd ordered, paid and tipped the waiter.

"Hungry?" he asked, setting the champagne bucket and food platter beside them on the night table.

"Maybe we should eat and get downstairs," Bailey suggested halfheartedly.

Steele shook his head. "We owe ourselves a time-out for love."

Needing no further persuasion, Bailey lifted the sheet invitingly. In the past, desire and passion had driven her into his arms, her body succumbing to the emotions her mind refused to acknowledge. This time, she came to him without reservation in her heart or mind. Steele's every touch reminded her they came together in an act of love, by its very nature an affirmation of the future.

THE ICE IN THE BUCKET had melted before they got around to opening the champagne. "To us," Steele toasted and handed her a glass.

"I'll go 'one more time' with you," Bailey added, ignoring the quiver of fear accompanying her brave words.

"We won't bust," he promised, giving her a reassuring kiss.

He propped the platter of fruits, cheeses and crusty French bread on her lap and popped a strawberry in her mouth. She rewarded him with a grape. They fed one another leisurely, lovingly, and, all too soon, the plate was empty.

They shared one last, long, champagne-flavored kiss, then rose and dressed to resume their masquerade.

NIGHT CLOAKED THE CASINO windows, seeming to increase the carnival atmosphere of the gaming rooms. Bypassing countless rows of slot machines, Steele guided Bailey to the highest stakes blackjack table.

Only one betting space was open. Steele took the stool, while Bailey arranged herself over his shoulder in a classic, Lady Luck pose. Not recognizing the dealer, a young blond woman, Bailey breathed a silent sigh of relief. Despite her confidence in her disguise, confronting people familiar with her or her sister unnerved her.

Five other players faced the dealer. Steele waited until they finished their round of play and the dealer called for new bets before joining. The name embroidered on the blonde's yellow satin shirt was Betty, and she welcomed

Steele while the players placed their chips on the "holes,"
the betting boxes painted on the green felt of the table.
After calling a waitress over to offer drinks, Betty dealt
the cards.

Steele introduced himself simply as Matt from Texas
and nodded at the other players, but kept his attention
on the cards to indicate he was a serious player. He ordered a soda water with a twist of lemon, too, rather than
an alcoholic beverage to give the same impression.

His playing, Bailey noted with pride, confirmed him
as a gambler who relied on skill rather than pure chance.
Her worries about his speed proved groundless. When
his winnings mounted, she saw the pit boss sharpen his
supervision of their table. She didn't need to look for a
name on his shirt. She knew him well; Hal was the boss
who'd offered Cliff extra time off to work the private
party.

Her skin prickled as if a sixth sense warned her of
danger. But when she saw him covertly signal the dealer
to shuffle more frequently, she knew he didn't suspect
their identities.

Shuffling was a house strategy to beat would-be card
counters. By keeping track of the high and low cards left,
expert counters could cut the house advantage by as
much as two percent, anathema to casino operators.

Knowing she, too, was under scrutiny, she was careful not to touch Steele or gesture while he was working
a hand. As an onlooker, she could bet on his cards, but
she couldn't offer advice—or signals—on how to play
them.

When shuffling failed to break Steele's winning streak,
Hal rotated dealers. The people who ran casinos, she
knew, were even more superstitious than the gamblers.

Cliff had told her about lucky and unlucky tables, and
she'd laughed when he'd described the penalty box where
"hot" dice used by winners at roulette or craps tables
were consigned until a pit boss determined they'd
"cooled."

Players dropped out when they saw "luck" running in
Steele's direction, while onlookers—with the antennae
peculiar to gamblers—sensed his streak and gathered
around the table to add their bets to his. Bailey claimed
a vacant stool when Steele, in true high-roller fashion,
filled the holes the departing players left open.

"You play it, honey," she cooed when he offered one
of his extra hands to her. "You're hot, tonight." She
smiled provocatively, and the crowd tittered at her double entendre.

Steele cocked a knowing eyebrow, glanced at his down
cards, told the dealer "One more time," then winked at
Bailey. She smiled back, but noticed the arrival of the
floor supervisor. He watched the play for endless moments, then said something to Hal. They turned and disappeared in the crowd.

Shortly afterward, a slender, impeccably groomed
man in a white linen suit worked his way to the front of
the crowd and dropped several fifty-dollar chips in a hole
Steele hadn't claimed. "Ray Hall," he said and sat down.
"Mind if I rub elbows?"

A gold tooth flashed when he smiled, but his blue eyes
were cold, Bailey observed. The sheen to his dark hair
told her he wore a hairpiece. It was a good one, though,
all-but-undetectable to an untrained eye.

"The more, the merrier," Steele agreed jovially, then
gave his name and shook hands. Like Steele, Ray didn't
drink or make conversation. He played consistently well,

but didn't latch onto Steele's streak, which was now just as much a result of luck as strategy.

Fed by the hypnotic slap of cards and click of chips, time sped by. Steele rotated a stiffening neck, and Bailey dutifully massaged his shoulders. Counting the high piles of chips in front of him, she realized his winnings were reaching the ten-thousand dollar mark, which would require him to produce identification for tax withholding.

Waiting for a lull in the play, she leaned over and whispered in his ear. "Cool it, or we'll have to file tax forms."

Steele patted her hand absently and assumed a slightly annoyed expression. "We'll eat in a few more minutes," he told her, then asked the dealer the time.

"Casino time," the dealer answered with a grin, holding up his hands to indicate he didn't wear a watch. He signaled for Hal, who told them it was close to midnight.

"How about doubling the stakes for one more round?" Steele asked him. "I'll give the house a chance to win back its money."

Bailey longed to kick him. They had their fake identification, but how could they lie to the Internal Revenue Service?

"I'll match him," Ray chimed in.

Hal hesitated, his broad face unsmiling. "I'll check with the supervisor," he said abruptly and strode away.

"Pit boss has the authority to raise the stakes," Ray told Steele. "You've got him nervous."

He's not the only one, Bailey added silently, hoping Steele knew what he was doing.

"Not much of a gambling house if they raise a ruckus about ten- or twenty-thousand," Steele drawled.

"You're used to Vegas?" Ray's question was casual, but his gaze sharpened. He was trying to place Steele, Bailey suspected, or learn more about his background to facilitate a check on him.

"Private games, back in Texas. My daddy didn't take to gamblin' much, so I had to keep my hobby on the quiet side 'til he passed on." He touched his Stetson briefly as if in respect for his father's memory, but he winked at Ray. "Found this little lady on my one visit to the Strip a few months back." He curled his arm around Bailey's waist and rested a possessive hand on her hip. "Only jackpot I hit on the trip."

Ray's cold gaze stripped her naked. Resisting the urge to cover the cleavage exposed by her plunging neckline, Bailey promised herself a hot shower when they returned to their room.

Hal returned with permission for Steele and Ray to double the stakes.

"Pocket change," Steele scoffed.

Pretending excitement, Bailey hugged him, then whispered in his ear. "Lose this one!"

"Gotta take care of the man handin' out the cards," he said, ignoring her and shoving a stack of chips across the table for the dealer, a tip large enough to crack the man's professional demeanor and make him blink in surprise.

The rest of the chips Steele divided into two piles. "This is it for me," he said, sliding the larger stack toward him, "and the rest is for the lady to play." He winked at her. "Go for it. You brought me luck, let's see how you do for yourself."

His grin told Bailey he'd planned to avoid the tax problem with this ploy from the start. Smiling her appreciation, she clapped her hands with delight. Ray claimed two betting holes. Feeling reckless, Bailey took the rest.

The dealer showed an eight as his up card. The light cast by the green-shaded, hanging lamp above them seemed to grow brighter, and the crowd of onlookers to fade into the deepening shadows around the table.

On the dealer's left, Ray initiated the play. For his first hand, he beckoned for two more cards, then slid them beneath the corresponding pile of chips. He studied his second two cards, signaled for another, then slid them under the next stack of chips.

Excitement hummed through Bailey's veins. She checked her first hand, then signaled the dealer to give her another. She hadn't gambled since her husband died and never for such high stakes. Barely lifting the edge of her new card, she glanced back at the dealer and said, "One more time," believing the phrase would give her luck.

It didn't. She busted. Flipping the three cards over, she gave Steele an apologetic look while the dealer raked in her chips. *Don't be superstitious,* she told herself. Just because she'd lost a hand when she'd used the phrase "one more time," didn't mean she'd lose Steele.

"Lucky in love, unlucky at cards," he reassured her.

A sense of foreboding nibbled at her nerves, nonetheless. She shivered, then blinked rapidly to defeat the threat of weak tears. Playing her second hand without exceeding twenty-one, she stayed with two cards on her third and split a pair of eights on the next, forcing her to buy more chips to stake the extra hand.

The dealer flipped over his down card; a six joined the eight already showing. He hit and drew a four for a count of eighteen. Ray lost his first hand, then beat the house with a nineteen on his second.

Rather than wait for the crowd's applause rewarding Ray's win to die down, Bailey happily flipped over her count of twenty. Steele kissed her, and the crowd added wolf whistles to their applause.

Despite her bust, her split left her three hands to play. Building the tension, she waited for the crowd to quiet before she announced, "Blackjack," and displayed her two-card hand. A jack and an ace, a "natural 21," paid her three-to-two odds. The crowd cheered, then groaned with sympathy when the first of her split eights' totaled less than the dealer's eighteen.

"Game's not over till the fat lady sings," Steele assured them.

The dealer swept those chips away. Bailey played her last hand—an eight, ten and a three for a second twenty-one, although not a natural.

Without waiting for the dealer to pay out, she hopped from her stool and wrapped herself around Steele as much from relief as the rush of winning. People crowded around them, congratulating and slapping them on the back. Reveling in the kiss she so badly needed, Bailey barely noticed.

"How about a drink to unwind?" Ray suggested when the crowd dwindled. "The oyster bar upstairs has a nice selection of snacks for the lady."

"On me," Steele insisted. Cashing in their winnings, they headed for the bar, where he ordered champagne and enough steamed clams, fried oysters and baked escargot to feed an army.

"Where do you hail from?" he asked Ray, who answered vaguely and deftly turned the questions on Steele. Bailey kept silent, figuring her role was decorative rather than informative. Whooping with laughter at one of Ray's jokes, Steele played the role of loudmouthed Texan well, while she struggled to smile.

Ray's expression, whenever he looked at her, went beyond a simple leer; it soiled her. Sex, for him, she suspected, would have more to do with power and degradation than pleasure. She hoped he was a lead to the private club and that she wasn't subjecting herself to his chilling company needlessly.

Yawning, she snuggled up to Steele in hopes of prompting Ray to make his move. Steele lifted an arm to her shoulders, but didn't pause in his conversation. She gave Ray another ten minutes, then began stroking Steele's thigh who tried, but failed, to ignore her.

"I think the lady's ready for bed," he told Ray. "It sure was a pleasure meetin' a fella card player." He signaled the waitress for the tab, then offered his hand to Ray. Bailey shuddered inwardly and decided to insist he wash it before he touched her.

"How long are you staying?" Ray asked. He'd already determined they had a room at the Sunburst.

Steele shrugged and pulled his money clip from his pocket. "Planned on a couple of days," he answered, dropping bills on the table. "But I'd expected a little more action. I might mosey on up to Vegas."

"What if I could get you an invite to a private game?"

Bailey wanted to applaud Steele's performance when he pretended to consider the question. "Stakes?"

"The sky's the limit." Ray grinned. "Or maybe I should say the green in your pocket."

"Sounds interestin'," Steele drawled. "Give me a ring in the mornin' and we'll see." He gave Bailey a lazy, seductive glance, then turned back to Ray and added, "But not too early."

11

THE TELEPHONE IN BAILEY and Steele's room rang shortly after noon the next day. Still in bed, they gazed at one another in a shared moment of anticipation mixed with disappointment at the end of their long night of loving.

Steele planted one last sweet kiss on Bailey's lips, then reached for the telephone. Her pulse pounding, Bailey rested her head on the pillow next to his, on the other side of the receiver. She'd barely identified Ray's oily voice, though, when Steele pulled away from her and slammed his hand on the bed.

Alarmed, she stared at him. He closed and opened his eyes and drew a deep, calming breath. "A helicopter, on the roof at eight o'clock? Sounds exciting!" His voice didn't betray his agitation, but Bailey could see the effort it cost him in the ripple of muscle in his cheek and the whitening of his knuckles on the receiver.

When Steele hung up, his eyes were wild. He glanced at the radio, which they'd set on an all-music station for privacy in case their room had been bugged while they were in the casino. He shook his head, clearly wanting more secrecy.

"We're checking out today, baby," he said in his Texas twang, then hurried her into the bathroom, where he turned the shower on full force.

"Ray's *the* one," he whispered.

"That's what we thought," she answered, confused.

He shook his head. "I mean the one who called and threatened to kidnap Kevin! I didn't realize it until I heard his voice on the telephone." He lifted his hands and curled his fingers in a choking motion.

"Calm down!" Bailey slipped her hands in his. "He'll lead us to Lana, and we'll put him in jail. Remember that when you look at him, or you'll give us away."

"I want to kill him," Steele growled.

Bailey wrapped her arms around him to soothe his fury—and to calm the rapid beating of her heart.

THE GLOW OF THE setting sun still fired the clear, desert sky as Steele and Bailey joined four other couples on the roof. Three were retirees, who immediately fell into a conversation centered on children and grandchildren, while the fourth was a young pair of newlyweds. Listening to them chatter excitedly about the private party, Bailey hoped they could afford the losses she felt certain they'd incur.

Ray joined them, escorting a tall, blond showgirl. Bailey recognized her as Dee-Dee, one of the clients who'd requested her at the salon and questioned her about Cliff's "accident." Dee-Dee's presence linked Ray to the deaths of her husband, son and brother-in-law as surely as his voice on the telephone identified him as the man who'd threatened to kidnap Kevin. Bailey could now more clearly understand Steele's violent reaction to his recognition of Ray's voice.

Steele shot Bailey a questioning glance and covered her hand with his. She'd dug her fingernails into his bicep, she realized. With conscious effort, she relaxed her grip. She didn't have to produce a smile or pretend politeness, though, when Dee-Dee purred up to Steele and tried to edge her aside. In a show of jealousy, she allowed all the hatred swelling within her to pour from her eyes and claw at the blonde's face.

"Meow," Ray muttered, pulling Dee-Dee back to his side.

"Chopper's coming." Steele defused the tension by drawing their attention to the sound of the distant but steady beat of a helicopter. A dark speck against the cloudless blue sky, it rapidly grew closer, whipping the hot, desert air into a raging wind as it settled on the roof.

Steele grabbed his Stetson. The shirred skirt of Bailey's leopard-print dress billowed at her hips.

Bailey stared at the black behemoth and thought of how isolated and vulnerable they'd be when they stepped within it. Gripped by sudden fear, she glanced behind her, toward the stairs leading down to the safety of the hotel.

A tall, dark-haired figure slipped through the lighted doorway of the vestibule and disappeared into the shadows.

Forrest.

Bailey snapped her head around to face the helicopter. Under the pretense of leaving a message for "Matt" at the front desk that afternoon, she'd handed Bonnie a note listing their arrival and departure times. Eyeing the name of a tour company and the white numbers painted on the chopper's side, she guessed Forrest would note them and initiate a search if they failed to return.

No matter what, vengeance would be hers.

Her courage revived, she climbed aboard the machine and claimed a window seat while Steele helped load the luggage. Night doused the fading embers of sunset when he joined her. The helicopter lifted straight up.

Fixing her sense of direction on the glow of the lights of Laughlin, she figured they were heading straight west when they left them behind, then south when the helicopter veered and a faint illumination lit the night to the east.

To the Dead Mountains.

THEY'D FLOWN WHAT seemed an eternity, but was barely ten minutes by Steele's watch, when flashing lights speared the darkness below them. The helicopter hovered, then slowly sank to the ground.

"Welcome to the Celestial Casino," Ray wisecracked over the microphone from his seat beside the pilot, "where the sky's the limit."

Burly men unloaded the luggage, while Ray led the group to a building constructed of adobe with long, low, rounded lines. Crushed stones covered its flat roof. Its design would make it look like an outcropping of rock from the air, Bailey suspected.

A tall man, thin to the point of emaciation and dressed in a black tuxedo, opened the large double doors. Smiling and ushering them inside, he introduced himself as Dieter Hawkins, the owner. With skin as white as his hair and eyes covered by tinted glasses, he reminded Bailey of a modern-day vampire. She shuddered and pressed closer to Steele, who dropped his arm around her shoulders.

"I'm so pleased you could join me in my humble gaming house," Dieter wheezed in a weak voice, "where the joys of dice and cards ban the mindless thunder of slot machines." He swept his arm in a graceful gesture to indicate the large hall behind him.

They stood on a railed landing with wide steps leading down into a lavishly decorated room. Dark walnut moldings matched the polished wood of the green felt-covered gaming tables and outlined walls draped in creamy velvet. Crystal chandeliers shimmered from the ceiling. Plush burgundy carpeting stretched across the floor.

Dieter led them around the tables to an equally elegant dining room. Delicious aromas rose from a burdened buffet table already crowded with diners. "As you can see, our other guests have arrived." He beamed at those who turned to greet him. "We'll get you settled so you can join them." He opened a door to a long hallway. "You'll find your suitcases outside your rooms." With an affable nod, he left them.

Their bedroom had its own bath, Steele and Bailey discovered, but otherwise wasn't much larger than a prison cell. "There's no radio or television," Bailey complained, dismayed at this limitation on their privacy.

"We're here to gamble," Steele reminded her in Matt's voice, then drew her into his arms and whispered, "We'll do our lovemaking in the shower." His kiss drugged her senses and soothed her nerves. "Get your primping done pronto, baby," he said loudly, raising his head and slapping her on the fanny. "I can't wait to get to those beautiful tables."

NEITHER STEELE NOR BAILEY had much appetite, but they forced themselves to eat. Dieter pushed drinks on them, which they accepted, then promptly set aside. When everyone had eaten their fill, their host opened the doors to the gaming room.

"Let the games begin!" he announced.

Noticing drapes pulled across the double doors and a microphone on the railed landing, Bailey exchanged a glance with Steele. "Are we going to have some entertainment?" he asked a dealer, selecting a blackjack table toward the back of the room, away from the stage. He claimed the seat to the dealer's left, as they'd planned, so he'd receive the first deal and allow Bailey to observe the other players without arousing suspicion.

"A lovely lady will sing for us at midnight," the man answered. Bailey was careful not to look at Steele. The singer, she was sure, would be Lana. Everything else had fallen neatly into place. Too neatly, she worried, again experiencing the sense of foreboding she'd felt when the helicopter had landed at the Sunburst.

Clinging to her composure, she smiled when the dealer introduced himself as Chuck. He was fair-haired with a lined, tanned face and a more hardened appearance than the dealers at the Sunburst. Glancing around the room, she didn't recognize any of the dealers or stickmen at the craps tables. If, as she suspected, Cliff had realized the games were fixed, Dieter may have stopped using honest dealers.

Claiming her attention, Chuck indicated she take the seat to Steele's left. "She's my good luck charm," Steele told him, "and doesn't play."

"We have more than enough tables and chairs for our guests," Chuck assured him and shot an admiring smile at Bailey. "With her beside you, you definitely can't lose."

"I couldn't agree more," Ray chimed in, joining them with Dee-Dee and and an older couple he introduced as Don and Kate. Short, round and gray-haired, they were brother and sister rather than husband and wife.

Dee-Dee took the stool to the dealer's right and pulled Don down next to her. "Let's sit woman, man, woman," she suggested with a tittering laugh. Don complied readily, seating his sister on his other side. Ray sat between Bailey and Kate.

"Shall we begin?" Chuck asked and unwrapped the cellophane from four decks of cards. Shuffling them, he set them facedown on the table and indicated Steele should cut. Watching closely when Chuck picked up the cards, Bailey eliminated the possibility of a stacked deck. No dealer's hands were fast enough to shift the cut and return the cards to their original position without distracting the players' attention.

"Place your bets," he called.

"Cautious tonight?" Ray taunted Steele when he dropped a fifty-dollar chip into his betting hole, but not Bailey's.

"Just want to get a feel for the table," Steele explained smoothly. "Why don't you go ahead and play the space?"

"Bad luck." Ray shook his head. "She's your woman."

Chuck dealt. Bailey admired his diamond pinkie ring as an excuse to watch his hands.

"Looks like you should buy the lady her own diamonds," Chuck told Steele. Bailey snapped her gaze to his face, afraid he'd sensed the true reason for her scrutiny.

"Made her leave 'em in the safe at home," Steele drawled. "No sense in asking for trouble."

"And I miss them." Bailey pouted, again letting her attention drop to Chuck's hands. As far as she could tell, he hadn't switched decks. Neither had she caught him second or bottom dealing or palming a card.

The hand could be quicker than the eye, though, especially an expert dealer's. Rather than risk arousing Chuck's suspicions any further, Bailey studied Steele's cards. Made from a high quality paper, they sported a baroque design of swirling colors.

Such an intricate pattern could be altered to allow for fine shadings, lines or cut-outs, while the border accommodated trim or edge work. The apparent newness of the cellophane-wrapped decks meant nothing. No law prohibited the manufacture of marked cards.

An hour's careful comparison of the face value of Steele's cards with the design on their backs confirmed her suspicion. The high-ranked cards were shaded slightly darker on the top, and the shading dropped lower with the value of the cards.

No one, however, seemed to take advantage of the marked cards. A wise move, Bailey thought. If a gambler started out losing, he'd be more likely to hedge his bets. This way, players gained confidence in their luck and continued to bet freely even in the face of a losing streak. How long, she wondered, before the game would shift?

Steele was doing well and expanded his playing to two hands, claiming Bailey's vacant betting hole, while the others steadily increased the size of their wagers. Dee-Dee played erratically, hitting or standing with no apparent strategy. Her incessant giggling annoyed Bailey to the point she could barely look at her. Ray and Don, however, seemed to think she was cute and encouraged her. Kate sipped steadily from the fresh drinks brought by an attentive, scantily clad waitress. Her giggles grew louder, too, and her playing deteriorated.

Steele played his more silent game, although he made a point of saying, "One more time," to request another card and then would glance at her significantly. Bailey smiled at him in return, but waited anxiously for what she considered Lana's inevitable appearance.

Despite the unqualified admission of love Steele had wrung from her, she still felt as if she were living on borrowed time. Lana was the mother of his child. What if she learned the error of her ways and, freed from her compulsive gambling, she again became Karen, the woman he'd loved?

Steele's luck turned, and Bailey snapped her attention back to the game. Don, she'd figured out, was a card counter, but his losses, too, began to mount. Ray continued to win and lose on a consistent basis. Forcing her attention to Dee-Dee, Bailey saw how the game was rigged.

The scheme was brilliant in its subtlety; the seating arrangement eliminated any need for the cooperation of the dealer. Dee-Dee's position gave her the last play before the dealer's and, reading the marked cards, she hit or stood depending on his hand, not hers. If he needed a low card, but the one on the top of the deck was high, she'd hit until the card he needed appeared. Conversely, she'd stand on a low hand if the next card were what he needed. The ploy failed if she busted quickly, yet worked consistently enough to raise the house advantage considerably. Since blackjack players played against the house and not one another, no one had any reason to suspect the dizzy blonde—or any of the other players sitting to the dealer's right. Glancing at the other blackjack tables, Bailey saw some were men. These appeared to drink heavily, always a convenient excuse for poor decisions.

Already established as a player who depended on chance rather than skill, Dee-Dee shrieked with laughter when she busted and scolded herself for cowardice when she came in low.

Bailey was sure that Ray could read the cards, too, but he was as vulnerable to Dee-Dee's manipulation as the other players.

Steele dropped back to one hand. "Until his luck returned," he explained to Ray. Don and Kate threw their money away as if the size of their bets could affect their cards.

Bailey allowed her attention to wander to the other tables. Marked cards probably rigged the poker games, too, but she wondered about the craps and roulette tables. Loaded dice? Not that it mattered. The marked cards were proof enough to call in the police.

Closing down the casino wasn't enough, though. She'd insist the police reopen their investigation of Cliff's accident. Its timing was more than coincidental. Why, though, was he allowed to return home if he'd seen through their scheme? And why hadn't he gone straight to the police instead of going on that camping trip?

Would she ever know?

AT MIDNIGHT THE HOUSE lights flickered, then dimmed to a single beam on each tabletop. A spotlight illuminated the stage. Bailey squeezed Steele's knee beneath the table, but Steele barely felt the comforting pressure. He lifted his gaze from the table and stared past Chuck at the blonde stepping through the drapes over the front door.

Dieter spoke into the microphone, introducing her as "Lady Luck."

Lana.

Automatically following the crowd's lead, Steele brought his hands together and joined the applause greeting her sequin-bedecked entrance. But shock clutched his mind.

Wolf whistles sounded through the room. To his eyes, though, Lana looked like hell. Once tanned and athletic, she was now pale and thin. Her face seemed to be all eyes, big and blue—and empty. Where was the joy he'd seen light her face whenever she performed?

Her naturally platinum hair looked as dry and lifeless as a bottled blonde's, where once its sheen had reflected the glow of the stage lights. Her collarbones jutted above the swell of her breasts, and her hip bones protruded against the cling of her tight-fitting evening dress.

She needed both hands to lift the microphone from its stand and stumbled when she descended the stairs to the gaming-room floor. Her voice was a whisper of its former full-throated range.

She looked as if her compulsion to gamble had consumed her from within, eating away her physical strength and inner vitality. She smiled and flirted with the men while she sang and passed through the tables but, to Steele, she looked like a puppet on a string, obeying the commands of an unseen master.

When she drew closer to his table, the empty expression in her eyes sharpened. She headed straight to him. Bailey slipped a possessive arm around his shoulders, but Lana dismissed her with a glance and halted beside him. He knew he should do something—anything—to shatter her concentration while she sang to him, but he was immobilized by the sight of the wrecked woman he'd once loved.

Bailey pinched the back of his neck—hard—and he gathered his wits, asking himself, what would Matt do?

Stretching his lips into a grin, he opened his arms and gripped the waists of both women. "Whoever said three's a crowd wasn't standin' in mah boots," he quipped in the heaviest twang he could summon.

His voice carried over the microphone and the crowd laughed. Lana ended her song, plucked the Stetson from his head and plopped it on her own. "How about a country and western tune for this hunk of a cowboy?" she asked, turning to the band on stage. She planted a kiss on Steele's cheek before she moved away and began to sing, still wearing his Stetson.

"If that doesn't bring me luck, nothing will." Steele addressed the table but his eyes were on Ray, studying his reaction. Ray's dark eyes were probing, as if seeking to see through Steele's disguise.

Had Lana recognized him? Steele swore inwardly, not knowing what to do. He wasn't the only man she'd sung to, but the reassurance failed to assuage his mounting worry.

In a show of jealousy, Bailey picked up a napkin to wipe Lana's lipstick from his face, but Steele reared away from her. "Don't mess with a kiss from a real Lady Luck," he snapped, clinging to his role. He bet big, swearing on Lady Luck's kiss.

He lost. When Lana left the room, still wearing his hat, he complained about losing that, too.

"She took a liking to you, she'll be back," Ray assured him, but Steele wasn't ready for another close encounter with his ex-wife. Neither did he like the glint of suspicion he saw in Ray's eyes.

"She's welcome to it," he said, standing and gathering up his few remaining chips. "Think I'll take a breather, though, while I've still got my shirt." Grasping Bailey's elbow, he guided her toward the drape-covered front doors. He would've preferred a less conspicuous exit, but had yet to see one and he had to get outside, had to find an escape route.

"She recognized you," Bailey said, confirming his worst suspicion when they moved away from the doors.

"How?" Not waiting for an answer, Steele hurried her around the corner of the building.

"I don't know. Woman's intuition, maybe. But we're in trouble."

At the sound of doors opening and closing behind them, he signaled Bailey to keep silent, then pushed her against the wall and stationed himself at the edge. Bailey slipped off her shoes and held the heels pointed out like weapons.

"Aim at their eyes," he whispered. She shuddered, but nodded.

A footstep crunched on the rock-strewn sand. Steele crouched, ready to spring.

12

"LANA!" THE NAME of his ex-wife slipped from Steele's lips as he grabbed the figure rounding the corner. Clapping a hand over her mouth, he held her against his chest, ready to thrust her into the arms of anyone who followed her.

No one appeared. "Are you alone?" he whispered. She nodded, and he shoved her away from him.

"Steele! I knew you'd come for me!" She threw herself at him. "I've been so afraid!"

"So you finger me and get us all killed!" He grasped her shoulders and peeled her off his chest.

"No, I didn't tell anyone!" She clutched the lapels of his western-cut jacket. "I've been hoping you'd come for me. I sing to every big man I see. Your disguise is good, but your hands . . ." She took them in hers. "I've never forgotten their size, their strength . . . their gentleness." She planted a kiss in his right palm. Steele jerked it from her grasp.

"I took your hat," she glanced at the Stetson she'd dropped on the ground when Steele grabbed her, "so I'd have an excuse to talk to you. Nobody else knows."

"How did you know where to look for us?"

"Ray said you went outside."

"Which means he won't be far behind." Bailey spoke for the first time. "We've got to get out of here."

"Who's she?" Lana demanded.

"A very special lady," Steele snapped, "and she's right. We don't have time for introductions. Is there a jeep or truck someplace?"

Lana shook her head. "Everything's flown in."

Steele repressed a curse. "We'll have to head for the hills."

"We won't last a day without water," Bailey objected. "We'll have to brave it out here." She turned to Lana. "You've got to go back in there. If you run into Ray—or if anyone asks why you followed us—tell him you were returning his hat. If he won't buy that, act embarrassed and admit you thought it was Steele, but you wanted to make sure before turning him in and causing a stir. I'll play the jealous shrew and accuse you of making a pass at my man. Understand?"

"But you have to get me out of here." Lana leaned against Steele's chest and sobbed against him. "I'll never gamble again. You were right, I was sick, but I've learned my lesson. Please, don't leave me!"

"The only way out is on the helicopter with the others!" Gripping Lana's shoulders, Steele pushed her away. "Don't you see?" He shook her for emphasis. "You've got to convince them you don't know me, or we'll all be killed. We'll notify the cops as soon as we get back to Laughlin."

"No! I can't stay here!" Tears streamed down Lana's cheeks. "They beat me! I want my baby, I want you!"

"Lana, please. We need you to be strong," Steele implored, but she went limp in his arms, forcing him to support her weight.

"It's no use, Steele." Bailey's voice was calm, but he detected an edge to it he'd never before heard. "What about a place to hide," she asked Lana, "where we can get water, clothes . . . like a laundry room, or something?"

"You mean you're alone?" Lana whimpered, swaying in Steele's grasp. "There's no one to help us?"

"Right." Steele glanced at Bailey, who was peering around the corner, on the lookout for Ray. "You know the place, we don't. Where can we go?"

At last, Lana seemed to recognize their plight. "This way." Steele snatched up his hat. She led them to the back of the building and eased open a door. The hum of machinery told him the room housed the generator supplying the building with electricity.

"Flashlight?" he asked, not wanting to turn on the light and lead Ray to them.

"Across the room. They keep one by every connecting door in case we lose power."

"Lock and move away from this door, carefully. Don't knock anything over."

With one hand on the wall, Steele felt his way through the blackness of the room toward the thin cracks of light outlining a door. He hit a shelf, and a bottle tipped, bouncing on his shoulder and sliding down his chest, where he caught it. Sweat dripped down his forehead and stung his eyes at the prospect of the door opening, either before or behind him, and a gunman splaying the room with bullets.

How could Lana have been so stupid to single him out?

Closing his mind to the thought before anger could make him careless, he reached the door and found the flashlight hanging by the light switch. He located and turned the lock, then aimed the beam close to the floor and examined the room.

As he'd thought, a huge generator squatted in the middle of the floor, while loaded shelves, industrial-sized refrigerators, washers and dryers lined the walls. Lana rushed to his side, but he shrugged her off and shone the light on Bailey, who was also studying the room.

The knob on the outside door rattled. She raised her stricken gaze to his. "Hide," he whispered, indicating the generator with the beam of the flashlight and pushing Lana in that direction. Rushing to the door, he switched off the flashlight.

"It's locked," he heard an unfamiliar voice say.

"Well, shoot it," Ray answered. "They got no place to run."

Plastering himself to the wall behind the door, Steele tensed for a loud blast, but heard, instead, the deadly whisper of a silencer. He heard, too, the beginnings of a scream, quickly muffled by a hand. Lana's scream and Bailey's hand, he figured.

The door opened slowly. He sucked in his breath, squeezing himself into the small space behind the door. The gunman reached inside and flicked on the light switch. Sliding the flashlight into his pocket, Steele, tense and ready to spring, gripped the doorknob.

"Hide and seek is over," Ray called from the doorway with a humorless chuckle. "Alley, alley, in come free."

Steele stared at the edge of the door, waiting for the men to step over the threshold, waiting for the gun to appear.

Glass suddenly shattered on the other side of the room. Ray and the stranger rushed through the doorway. Shoving the door with every ounce of his weight, Steele rammed it against Ray's shoulder, knocking him aside and lunging for the other man's gun hand.

He missed the gun, but whipped the man's arm upward and slammed him against the wall. The gun clattered to the floor. Steele yanked the man around and slammed him into Ray, pinning both men to the wall.

Ray fired his gun. The shot went wild, but he twisted his wrist and aimed at Steele.

"Drop it!" Bailey's shout accompanied the whistle of the silencer. A bullet thudded into the door by Ray's head. As the gun slipped from his fingers, Steele caught it.

"Nice shot," he complimented Bailey, eyeing the bullet hole less than a foot from where his own head had been. "Keep those arms up," he told the men, shoving them forward and frisking them. "Where'd you learn how to shoot?" he asked, glancing at Bailey.

"Cliff." She stood with her knees slightly bent, her arms extended, the gun held in both hands. Not a quiver betrayed a hint of nervousness. She stared at Ray.

Lana appeared from behind the generator. "Take off your pantyhose," Steele told her, "and find anything else I can use to tie up these thugs." Lana hurried to a stack of laundry bags and pulled out the cords.

"You won't get away, you know," Ray said when she brought the items to Steele. "The desert will kill you, if Dieter doesn't."

"Like he killed Cliff Richards?" Bailey demanded. She sauntered toward Ray, rolling her hips provocatively. With her breasts swelling above the low bodice of her leopard-print dress and the shirred skirt accentuating the curve of her narrow waist and rounded hips, she appeared to be all luscious, enticing woman—save for the gleaming barrel of the gun she aimed at Ray.

Ray paled. From recognition of the name or fear of Bailey, Steele wasn't sure.

"Remember him?" Bailey asked, her voice a velvet caress. "An honest dealer, who didn't like to cheat people."

Ray stared at the end of the gun, but made no answer. Finished tying up the other man, Steele pulled Ray's hands behind his back.

"On your knees," Bailey commanded. Ray looked at Steele.

"I'd do what the lady says," Steele advised. Trembling, Ray lowered himself to his knees without taking his frightened gaze from Bailey's gun.

"But you didn't trust him to keep his mouth shut, did you?" Her voice was still a seductive whisper. "So, somehow, you arranged to run his truck off the road, a truck that also contained an innocent, prospective father." Her voice hardened now, and she pressed the nozzle of the gun against Ray's temple. "And a four-year-old boy...my son."

She cocked the trigger. Ray closed his eyes. Tears joined the sweat pouring from his face. Steele stepped forward, worried Bailey might go too far. He wouldn't begrudge her revenge, but knew she couldn't live with cold-blooded murder on her conscience. Bailey shook her head, warning him not to interfere.

"How did you do that, Ray?" Soft, sweet and scary, her voice was back in control. Steele prayed she was, too.

Ray shuddered. "I had nuthin' to do with it," he blubbered, opening his eyes. "I swear on my mother's grave!"

"Who, then, Ray? And how?"

"Dieter! The dealer said he didn't feel good and wanted to go home, but Dieter didn't trust him. He let him go because he came with some other dealers from Laughlin. Hal, the pit boss who sent him, knew he was going camping and where. Dieter sent the chopper after him. I had nuthin' to do with it!"

"How do we escape, Ray? Tell me that, and I won't kill you."

"Dirt bikes, in the next room. Door's hidden behind the linen cabinet over there." He rolled his eyes to the right. "Key's in my left pocket."

Bailey lowered the gun, and Ray sagged with relief. Steele found the keys, tossed them to Bailey, then gagged the men with pillowcases.

Steele whistled at the arsenal the room contained. He longed to blow it up, but didn't want to risk harming innocent people. Besides, their time was growing short. Someone might come looking for Ray. Selecting a semi-automatic, he filled his pockets with ammunition, then grabbed a foam fire extinguisher from the wall and sprayed the rest of the weaponry.

Bailey and Lana pushed three bikes to the door in the other room, while he smashed the engines of the extra ones.

"Empty some of those liquor bottles and fill them with water," Bailey told Lana. "I'll see if I can find us clothes to protect us from the sun."

Steele locked Ray and the other man in the hidden room, then joined the women. Bailey told him to wrap the water bottles in towels and stuff them into laundry bags, while she and Lana changed into dealer uniforms, tuxedo shirts and black men's pants. "We'll tie the bags to our backs," she explained, "like backpacks and hope the bottles don't break."

When they were ready, Steele quickly showed Lana how to operate the dirt bikes. Bailey had ridden such bikes as a teenager and offered to take the lead. He agreed and she roared out the door, guiding the way into the darkness of the Dead Mountains.

BAILEY HEADED NORTH, in hopes of finding a trail to the more familiar mountains directly west of Laughlin. Cliff had been an avid outdoorsman, and she'd accompanied him on numerous hikes and four-wheel drive trips. She was no novice to desert survival and, once in familiar terrain, she was sure she could find safety. Dieter, she figured, would expect them to flee eastward, toward the more populated Colorado River area.

As soon as she rounded a jagged outcropping of rock large enough to block them from view of the casino, she flicked on her headlight. Steele pulled up beside her, protesting.

"We've got to be able to see," she insisted. "If we hit a rock or a cactus, we could puncture a tire or hurt ourselves. We need to make time until they figure out what happened. If we hear the helicopter, we'll do without the headlights."

Steele nodded. "This is your country, you call the shots." With a loving pat on her back, he indicated she retain the lead.

Longing for a trail, but finding none, Bailey stuck to hillsides to avoid the danger of running into either a precipice or a box canyon. Surrounded by the deepest dark of the hours after midnight, her world narrowed to the sphere illuminated by her headlight—an eerie, foreign world. Rocks and desert shrubs appeared without warning, looming with sudden menace. The pointed leaves of yuccas looked like spears, Joshua trees like lurking monsters and creosote bushes like crouched creatures.

The sky slowly brightened to the east, heralding dawn and stirring desert animals to life. Shadows moved, usually beyond the range of her headlights, but she glimpsed the white behinds of pronghorn antelope fleeing her noise and the reflected red of a curious coyote's eyes.

Recognizing the pale diamond pattern of a Mohave rattlesnake crossing her path and disappearing up the hill, she halted abruptly. Her fear of pursuit had blinded her to this danger. Steele and Lana, their faces streaked with dust, drew up beside her. "Water stop," Bailey said, waiting to mention the snake until she could speak calmly.

She eyed the area carefully before dismounting and pulling a water bottle from Lana's pack. "We need to spread out," she said while they drank. "Snakes are active this time of day, and we could come up on one fast. If the first bike startles it, and it doesn't have time to move away, it might strike at the second bike."

"Rattlesnakes?" Lana asked, her face paling at Bailey's nod.

"If you see one, don't panic," Bailey told her. "Snakes want to avoid you as much as you do them. Stop or swerve, if you can, but remember a snake can only strike half its length."

Lana moaned and almost dropped the water bottle. Steele took it from her.

"We'll travel another couple of hours, then find some shade and rest during the heat of the day." Finishing the water, Bailey stowed the bottle back in Lana's bag. "Wait until I signal before you follow, then keep that distance from me at all times." She turned to Steele. "I'm going to start winding down the mountain and heading east." She lowered her voice. "I'm hoping to find some shelter. We're sitting ducks for a chopper out here." He nodded and curled a hand around her neck, pulling her close for a kiss.

Aware of Lana's scrutiny, Bailey slipped away from him and mounted her bike, but she couldn't escape the doubts crowding her mind so easily.

Was she now living as well as playing the role of Steele's mistress?

THE SUN BROKE FREE of the horizon, washing out the rosy hues of dawn with white heat. Creating switchbacks to descend the mountainside in large loops, Bailey strained to see a spot of green in the open, gravelly plain below them, but all she saw was scattered creosote bushes, bursages and yuccas stretching toward the next rise.

She halted when they reached the plain, but while she debated whether or not to cross it, she heard the steady thumping rotors of an approaching helicopter.

13

BAILEY GLANCED frantically to her right and left. Certain they'd never beat the helicopter across the flat open plain, she headed for the base of an arroyo that the infrequent but heavy desert rains had carved into the mountainside.

No welcome splash of green fed by underground water greeted her eyes, but a wide ledge of rock protruded from the hillside, the sandy earth around and below it washed away by runoff. Dismounting, she cautiously pushed the bike into the shade ahead of her.

"Hurry!" Lana urged, coming up behind her. Bailey shook her head, aware of the throb of the approaching helicopter rising in volume, but the J-shaped tracks in the sand warned her to listen for another danger. One more step, and she heard it—a dry rattle.

They weren't the only ones to seek sanctuary from the sun. An innocent-looking mound of sand shifted as a sidewinder lifted its horned head from its resting coil.

"Get back!" she yelled. Lana's bike crashed behind her, but Bailey didn't turn.

The thunder of the helicopter grew louder. "Shoot it!" Lana begged.

"It can still bite by reflex after it's dead," Bailey shouted. She pushed her bike toward the snake, revving the engine and stamping her feet in hopes the vibrations would goad the sidewinder into retreating. Its rattle an angry buzz, it raised its head higher in a striking pose.

A rock sailed past her, landing just short of the snake. It lunged.

"Don't risk your bike," Steele said, handing her some of the stones he'd collected.

"Keep them on this side of it," she told him, tossing one to demonstrate. "Otherwise, it'll feel cornered and stay to defend itself."

Steele obeyed. Faced with their steady barrage of rocks, the sidewinder uncoiled and slithered away in its looping, sideways fashion.

The thumping of the helicopter's rotors was almost upon them. Bailey shoved her bike all the way beneath the ledge, then turned to help Steele with the other two. Lana stood rooted in the sun, her gaze glued to the departing rattler.

"Come on!" Steele grabbed her arm and hauled her into the shade. Wrapping her arms around his neck, she collapsed against him, shaking with terror. Bailey untied the laundry bags from their backs, then slipped off her own.

The helicopter roared overhead, its shadow rippling across the plain in front of them. They pressed their backs into the rock. The chopper hovered, then circled the area three times before moving eastward.

Bailey slowly slid down to sit on the ground. Drawing her knees to her chest, she hugged them with her arms and lowered her head. Lana still clung to Steele. Envying her the comfort of those strong arms and broad chest, Bailey drew long, steadying breaths.

"Cut it out, Lana!" Steele's voice was harsh. Bailey looked up to see him push his ex-wife away. "This is all your damned fault! How can you expect sympathy from me?" Visibly trembling, Lana sank to the ground.

"Hold her, Steele," Bailey said dully, numbing herself to the pain of her words. "If she falls apart, we'll never make it out of here."

Turning his back on Lana, he squatted down next to Bailey. "Are you all right?" He stroked her cheek.

Bailey bit her lip, longing to crawl into his arms and release her fear and tiredness in a torrent of calming tears. "I'm fine," she said, staring out at the plain. "Take care of your wife."

"*Ex*-wife," Steele corrected. Lana gasped.

"We need to drink some water." Bailey dropped the subject. "Then sleep." Her eyes felt gritty; she removed her contact lenses. Steele did the same.

"I'm sorry." Lana edged closer to Steele when he passed her the water bottle. "I never meant for this to happen." Steele stared straight ahead of him, not looking at her.

Lana talked faster. "I begged Dieter not to involve you, not to ask you for the money. I swore I'd pay him back, if he'd only let me go back to work in Vegas. I didn't tell him about you or Kevin. He found your pictures in my wallet...." Her eyes filled with tears, but she fought them. "And he had Ray beat me up. Ray enjoys other people's pain." She shuddered. "If I didn't do what I was told, Dieter threatened to let him have me for a night."

Pausing, she reached out and touched Steele's arm. "I never meant to hurt you or Kevin...please, believe me."

"Like you didn't mean to hurt us when you took Kevin's trust fund and threw it away on the roulette wheel?" Steele turned to her. Bailey couldn't see his face, but she recognized the bitterness in his tone and saw Lana's struggle to absorb it.

"I've made a lot of mistakes," Lana admitted with sad dignity, "and letting you and Kevin go was the biggest one." Handing him the water bottle, she lay down and turned her back to him.

Steele swung around to Bailey. "This doesn't change my feelings for you."

Bailey studied the face she'd come to love whether it was bearded or clean-shaven, blond or red-headed, blue-eyed or hazel. "Now isn't the time to discuss it," she said simply. Steele's jaw tightened with anger, and he parted his lips to argue.

"Surviving the day in a hundred-plus-degree desert has to be our first priority," she added quickly, speaking loud enough for Lana to hear. "Talking increases water loss."

Steele mouthed the words, "I love you."

"Keep your mouth closed and breathe through your nose," she advised, glancing away from him.

As the mother of his child, didn't Lana deserve a second chance? But, now that she'd decided to take a gamble on a new life, how could she bear to lose it?

"The ground can be as much as thirty degrees warmer than the air," she went on doggedly, focusing her mind on survival, "but we have to rest. Lie parallel to the back wall, where the soil will be the coolest. No matter how hot you get, don't take your outer clothes off. The fabric will hold in moisture." Lana sat up and moved to lie down where Bailey indicated.

The wall was only long enough for two to lay head to head. Not sure she could sleep, Bailey offered to take first watch, but Steele insisted he would.

"Sit on a bike," she told him, "and keep drinking water. Don't try to conserve it. Each of us needs to drink at least a gallon throughout the day."

Bailey laid her head next to Lana's. Whose head would share Steele's pillow in the future? she wondered. Lana was seriously weakened both emotionally and physically by her ordeal, but what would she be like once she recovered?

Her dignity in the face of Steele's hostility showed character. A rehabilitation program would teach her to overcome her compulsion to gamble, the weakness that had driven Steele away from her. Her faded beauty would return with her health, and she'd regain self-respect with a willingness to face her mistakes.

She'd again be Karen, the mother of Steele's child, the woman he'd loved and married.

Plagued by anxiety, Bailey dozed fitfully for half the day, then rose to change places with Steele. They let Lana rest. Before Steele lay down, Bailey accepted his kiss, unable to deny herself the comfort of his touch, but she refused to discuss their future.

If any of them had one. Her stomach rumbled with hunger no matter how much she filled it with water. Self-doubt gnawed at her. Would she be able to find a way out of the mountains? Could they make it through another dark ride in the unforgiving desert?

Periodically she heard the whirr of the helicopter in the distance, but didn't see it. When at last the sun relented and sank toward the horizon, she buried her fears and turned to wake Lana and Steele. Gazing at their heads so close together, she paused. Did they belong together?

Rather than answer the question, she shook them gently. Lana's face was drawn and haggard, despite her rest. She didn't complain, though, while they drank their fill of water and silently packed the bottles.

Feeling none too well herself and realizing the weaker woman had to feel even worse, Bailey praised her. "You're doing fine," she assured her when they mounted their bikes. "Hang in there. We'll make it."

Lana smiled wanly, but tired tears glazed her blue eyes. "If I slow you down," she glanced at Steele, who kept his face turned away, "leave me behind. He's right. This is all my fault. I shouldn't have followed you outside, or I should've listened to you and faced Ray—"

"Listen," Bailey interrupted, rolling her bike next to Lana's. "You were in a bad situation and at the end of your rope. I might've done the same thing in your shoes. For that matter, Steele and I should've stayed at the blackjack table. We're not leaving you behind. We're going to make it, and we're going to make it together. Got that?"

Lana nodded and wiped her eyes, then straightened her shoulders determinedly. Bailey patted her on the back, then set out across the plain, her own resolve strengthened by her words.

While she rode, she thought of Bonnie, waiting and worrying at home. If she'd listened to her, she wouldn't be fighting for her life in the desert. Remembering other times she'd ignored her sister's cautious counsel, she also remembered how Bonnie always had stood by her. Could she help her now?

For the first time, she consciously telegraphed a message to her twin. They'd never actually communicated with words, sensing feelings and images instead, so Bailey opened herself to her fear and sent it out through the gathering dark.

Gradually, she felt a measure of calm seep into her soul. Was the feeling Bonnie's answer? She didn't know, but she welcomed its lingering solace as the hours passed.

The helicopter still prowled the sky, stabbing the mountains with its spotlight. Their progress slowed to a walk because of the need to seek shelter whenever the helicopter neared and fear of detection if they used their headlights.

The rise of the crescent moon assured Bailey they were headed east and north. When it climbed high in the sky and a faint glow still lingered on the horizon, she dared to hope what she saw was a reflection of the lights of Laughlin. Rather than risk raising Steele and Lana's hopes only to shatter them, she kept silent until she topped a rise and spotted the short strip of illuminated buildings in the distance, a tiny oasis of neon in the vastness of the dark desert. A ragged cheer tore from her dust-laden throat.

"I knew you could do it!" Steele halted his bike next to hers and hugged her. Lana sobbed with relief.

"I wasn't so sure," Bailey admitted, and Steele laughed.

Laughing with him, she felt tears of strain slide down her cheeks. "We're not home yet, though," she added, sobering and wiping her cheeks. The rosy fingers of dawn poked at the horizon beyond Laughlin and they still had miles to go...miles through open, sandstone hills...miles exposed in morning light.

They'd never beat the sun to town.

One swoop of the chopper, three rifle shots and they'd be dead. Even as her mind acknowledged that they had no choice but to take cover again and endure another long day of desiccating, debilitating heat, Bailey also realized how little water they had left. When night again shrouded the white hot sun, would they have the strength left to mount their bikes?

Fear and dread swept through her, seeming to narrow her choices to how she would die—slowly from thirst and dehydration or instantaneously from a bullet on a suicidal run for town.

Squeezing her eyes closed, she drew a deep, calming breath, then looked around her to get a firm fix on her bearings. Directly north of them and west of Laughlin, lay the more familiar contours of Newbury Mountain. Tucked within one of the many canyons was a tiny, perennial stream shaded by salt cedar, seepwillow, reeds and rushes. They could lie in the shallow water to cool their bodies and even risk drinking it when they ran out of their own water. Unless . . .

Bonnie, send help, she prayed, picturing in her mind the stream-fed canyon they'd visited with their husbands.

She turned away from the lights of Laughlin without conferring with Steele or Lana. There was no time for discussion. To find the canyon before the helicopter found them, they still had to race against the rising sun.

They almost made it.

Just as they reached the familiar trail leading into the water-fed canyon, they heard the faint beat of the helicopter rotors. Narrow and winding, the trail hugged the cliff face, providing no margin for error and no protection from bullets.

With no cover in sight, they had no choice but to chance it. Bailey glanced back, past Lana, for one, last, fortifying look at Steele. Then, she headed down the trail, the roar of the other bikes close behind her—but not loud enough to block the sound of the machine pursuing them.

Its shadow engulfed them in darkness, the thunder of the rotors deafening as it hovered, then swooped, whipping the air into a frenzy of blinding dust and grit. Bailey fell to her left, toward the safety of the rock wall, away from the yawning drop of the canyon.

Scrambling to her feet, she pressed her back against the wall. The black, glass-enclosed bubble of the helicopter faced her, then veered away, as if to slash her with its runners before it rose and disappeared from view.

Glancing at the trail behind her, she saw Steele help Lana crawl from under her dirt bike, then they edged toward her, Steele in the lead. "Lost the semiautomatic," he confessed disgustedly and took her hand. They sidled downhill, against the wall, still fighting to reach the canyon floor.

If they made it, and the helicopter landed, all they had were two handguns and however many bullets they contained to defend themselves.

The black helicopter swooped at them again...and again. Bailey wondered why their pursuers didn't just shoot them, then realized their deaths, like Cliff's, were to appear accidental.

Inch by agonizing inch, they felt their way down the winding trail, blinded and deafened by the chopper's attacks. Her husband and son's deaths, Bailey prayed, hadn't been so prolonged. Caught on a more open road, Cliff hadn't had a chance. She now realized that the dents in the roof of the truck could've been caused by the chopper's runners rather than the wreck.

Although smaller than the helicopter that flew them to the casino, this one still couldn't dive far between the narrowing walls of the canyon. Would they give up, then, and shoot?

A shot rang out, as if to answer her question, but no bullet ricocheted off the rock near them. The trail widened when they neared the canyon floor. Steele urged her into a run, pulling Lana behind him.

Rounding a bend, Bailey stumbled to a stop at the sight of a red jeep parked at the end of the trail. "Trapped! We're trapped!" she screamed. She spun around to face Steele. Defeat drained the adrenaline fighting her exhaustion. She swayed.

Still running, he urged her forward with his free hand. "Where can we go?" Bailey sputtered. Then she saw where his gaze was fixed. Forrest stood a few meters away behind a large boulder, a rifle on his shoulder. He took careful aim at the helicopter. He fired. Bonnie's dark head popped up next to him, but Forrest pushed her back down.

No longer needing Steele's prodding to lift her tired legs, Bailey rushed toward her twin. "You heard me, you're here!" she cried. She stumbled into her sister's arms, and they sank together onto the ground behind the boulder.

Forrest tossed Steele another rifle, and Lana collapsed in a heap next to Bailey. "I was right," Bailey babbled, aware of no one but her twin, "they killed Cliff and Travis and Ron. They ran them off the road with a helicopter just like they tried to do to us."

Soothing her with soft words, Bonnie held her, but Bailey couldn't stop; the story spilled from her.

Bonnie had known something had gone wrong, known it in her bones.

All through the long day Bailey had spent in the desert, the mountains on the Nevada side of the river had drawn her eyes. Forrest had discounted her foreboding, assuring her she only suffered from worry. When dusk fell, though, cold fear had gripped her. She'd trembled with it and insisted he go with her to Bailey's house, where she'd stood on the back deck and stared at the jagged, desert mountains on the other side of the river.

"Go rent a four-wheel-drive," she'd told Forrest. The force of her conviction had convinced him to obey without question. When he was gone, she'd returned her gaze to the desolate hills and told her sister, "I'm here. I'm ready."

Forrest had spent the night with her at Bailey's house, where she'd woken at dawn with the image in her mind of the stream-fed mountain canyon she'd frequented with her twin and their husbands. Breaking into Cliff's locked gun cabinet, they'd taken his hunting rifles. She'd also persuaded a friend on the police force to accompany them.

"We left him at the end of the gravel road," she told Bailey, "his car couldn't make it all the way here. He'll hear the gunfire and radio for backup. They'll catch these murderers—" she squeezed Bailey's ribs "—all because of you!"

Bailey lifted her head. "I might not have made it without you. I swear I'll never call you chicken again!"

"Chicken?" Lana echoed in disbelief. "If I had half the courage of either one of you, none of this would've happened."

"You have it." Bailey turned and grasped her hands. "You've faced your mistakes, and now you have the chance to rectify them."

"How?"

"Testify against Dieter and Ray."

"Oh, I'll do that, all right," Lana swore. "I'll see those two put away for a long time."

Disengaging herself from Bonnie, Bailey hugged Lana. They were only vaguely aware that the firing had stopped and that another helicopter, bearing the word Police, had arrived.

"I've lost him to you, haven't I?" Lana asked, pulling from Bailey's embrace.

Bailey didn't have to ask who she meant—Steele, the man who'd bullied his way into her heart and promised her a new future.

She looked into Lana's face, bruised with exhaustion, misery and regret. Kevin's mother's face.

"No," she said, "he's yours."

14

"WHAT?" STEELE REACHED down, hauled Bailey to her feet and hustled her farther into the canyon, away from the others. "Did I hear you right?" he asked, stopping behind the green curtain of a tall salt cedar. "You're handing me over to Lana, like I'm a piece of used furniture?"

Bailey cupped his face with her hands, stroking his beard with her fingers, trying to tame his temper with her touch. "She's the mother of your son," she said. "For Kevin's sake, you owe her a second chance."

Steele jerked his head away from her. "She turned her back on both of us."

"And she regrets it," Bailey countered softly, dropping her hands to her sides. "She was sick and couldn't help herself. Are you going to punish her for the rest of your lives?"

"I'll help her, Bailey. I'll see she gets counseling and let her visit Kevin. Hell, if she wants to teach aerobics again, I'll even give her a job. But I don't love her, I love you! Do you think I can turn my emotions on and off like a water spigot? Can *you?*"

Bailey winced, knowing she had to lie. "How long have we known each other? A little over a month?" She fixed her gaze on the small stream, unable to continue if she looked at Steele. "A month away from your home, a month when you've been worried about the life of your son and known what happened to mine. Danger and tragedy brought us together, Steele. Lana will testify against Dieter and Ray. Kevin's safe now, and you can go back to your life in Connecticut, a life where Lana belongs and I don't."

"Karen belonged to that life," he argued. "Lana didn't and never will. Haven't you ever heard the expression, 'you can't go home, again?' You're a part of my life now, and I want you to be a part of my life in the future!" He wrapped his fingers around her upper arms and pulled her close to him.

"Karen and Lana are one and the same," Bailey persisted, staring at the broad chest where she'd never again lay her head. "You loved the woman you knew as Karen. Lana can be that woman, again—if you give her the chance. How could I take that chance away from her?" She looked into his face, begging him with her eyes to understand, to stop making what she had to do harder than it was. "I know what it's like to lose a husband and son. How can I do that to another person?"

"She lost me before I ever met you." He released her suddenly, and she stumbled back a step. "You're using her as an excuse to cling to the past and live with the ghosts of your husband and son."

The anger in his blue eyes scorched her, hotter than the sun beating down on her head. Unable to bear the sight, Bailey turned her back on him to return to the others gathered around the jeep.

"You're a coward!" Steele yelled after her. "Afraid of the future!"

She flinched, but kept on going. He would understand—in time. She was doing the right, the honorable thing, by returning Steele to his family.

Why, then, did it hurt so much?

SHE WASN'T A COWARD, Bailey told herself in the ensuing hours as Steele, Lana and she gave the police their preliminary reports and submitted to the medical examinations Bonnie insisted they have. What could take more courage than facing a future without Steele?

Being alone with him, she realized. They left Lana, who showed signs of severe exhaustion and dehydration, at the hospital and Forrest drove them toward her house. Bonnie planned to fix them something to eat, then tuck them into bed.

Steele hadn't spoken to her since he'd called her a coward, but the other couple didn't appear to notice. They plied them with questions about the casino and their ordeal. Once at home and in the shower, Bailey wondered if he would renew their argument when they were alone. But her biggest concern was: could she send him back to Lana if he touched her?

She didn't know. And she wouldn't have to find out. After they ate, Steele asked Forrest to take him to a motel. "This house is a shrine to the dead," he explained in the face of Bonnie and Forrest's surprise. "I can't sleep here."

The bitterness in his voice sliced through Bailey. She'd heard that note in his voice before—when he spoke of Lana. How quickly his love could turn to hate....

Bonnie shot her a worried glance and sat down beside her, but Bailey shook her head slightly, warning her to keep silent and promising to explain later.

Steele quickly packed his and Kevin's clothes, then the boy's favorite toys. The rest, he said, he'd arrange to have shipped to Connecticut. When he was finished, he stalked out the front door without saying goodbye.

"It's better this way." Bailey gently eased Forrest and her sister out the door after him. "He belongs with his family, not me."

"Sounds to me like the two of you need some sleep," Forrest said. "Neither of you is making any sense."

Bailey nodded and rummaged through her depleted resources to summon a smile. Sleep wouldn't change her decision, but she'd welcome its escape from her thoughts and feelings.

When she was alone, exhaustion drove her to her bedroom, but she halted in the doorway when she saw her bed unmade, the pillow still bearing the imprint of Steele's head. Moaning, she dashed into her son's room, flung open the closet door and pulled the battered rabbit from its shelf. Hugging it to her breasts, she curled up on the bottom bunk, but a hard lump pressed into her ribs. Digging beneath her, she pulled out one of Kevin's tiny trucks.

She clutched it until the metal bit into her palm, then she opened her hand and brought it to her lips. She kissed the rabbit, too, then gently laid the toys on the pillow and left the room.

When she returned, she carried a gift box. With loving hands, she wrapped the toys in tissue, set them in the box and stowed the package on the closet shelf. Tomorrow, she would follow her sister's oft-repeated advice to turn her son's bedroom into an anonymous guest room.

She would not live with ghosts, as Steele had accused but, today, she would sleep with Steele's memory. She'd lay her head on the pillow that had held his and wrap herself in his sheets, in his scent—just one more time.

WHEN BAILEY AND Bonnie's parents returned from Disneyland with Jenny and Kevin, Steele collected his son, picked up Darby from Bonnie's and returned to Connecticut with Lana. Forrest, however, remained behind.

He was opening a security firm in Laughlin.

The police investigation into Dieter's club had led to the discovery of a conspiracy extending beyond the Sunburst. Casino employees throughout Laughlin had been bribed into directing Ray to big bettors for invitations to the private parties, and the casino owners were beefing up their internal security—a need Forrest intended to meet to support his new family.

He and Bonnie had decided to get married and he planned to adopt Jenny.

Bailey had never felt more alone. She wouldn't dim her sister's happiness by discussing how much she missed Steele . . . how empty the house seemed when she came home from work and only Max was there to greet her . . . how her gaze would fall on the kitchen table and she'd remember the night they'd played "strip" blackjack . . . how she'd sit on the glider on the deck and long for the weight of his arm across her shoulders.

Fighting the pain, she kept busy. She stripped the baseball posters from Travis's room and painted the walls a pale yellow. She gave his toys to charities, save for the softball gloves, which joined his rabbit and Kevin's truck in the gift box on the closet shelf. The bunk beds, she sold, replacing them with a double bed covered in a cheerful daisy print.

She cleared off the bookshelves, pulling the photographs from their frames and storing them in photo albums. Allowing herself one momento, she took the picture of Cliff, Travis and her from the nightstand drawer and set it on her dresser. They were a part of her past, loved and never to be forgotten.

She didn't have a picture of Steele and Kevin but, these two she had to forget.

AUGUST MELTED INTO September. Forrest returned to New York to sell his condominium apartment and ship his belongings to Bonnie's. Their wedding was scheduled for October, when the heat cooled. They planned a simple affair, an outdoor ceremony by the river in Bailey's backyard.

"You'll be my maid of honor, of course," Bonnie said one day while they sat on Bailey's back porch and made plans. "And—" she paused "—Forrest wants Steele to be his best man."

Bailey rose and wrapped an arm around a porch post. She stared at the mountains across the river. She'd known she'd see Steele and Lana when they returned to testify at Dieter and Ray's trials, but a court date had yet to be set.

She'd thought she'd have more time, time to forget.

"Has he said he'll come?" she asked.

"Yes."

Bailey leaned her forehead against the pillar. "Will Lana be with him?" She wished them happiness, but she couldn't bear to see them together.

"Forrest didn't say. She's in counseling and teaching aerobics in Steele's gym, but they're not married."

"Yet," Bailey whispered.

IN HER CAUTIOUS FASHION, Bonnie planned two wedding rehearsals. As the flower girl, Jenny was to walk with

Kevin, the ring bearer. Bonnie worried she'd wander off when she recognized friends attending the service.

Wanting to limit her time in Steele's presence, Bailey argued. How would an extra rehearsal without guests make a difference?

After two rehearsals, Bonnie responded, Jenny would have her destination, the canopy erected in Bailey's yard for the service, clear in her mind. She didn't want to spoil her processional by chasing or calling after her daughter.

Knowing she and her sister shared the same streak of stubbornness, Bailey subsided. Bonnie deserved to have her wedding day the way she wanted it. She silently cursed her, though, when Steele and Kevin stepped through her front door.

The boy's happy greeting allowed her to stretch her smile to include Steele when she welcomed them. His hair was again blond and he was clean-shaven. He noted that she'd dyed her hair back to its original dark color, but she sensed he felt as awkward as she did.

"Where's Lana?" she forced herself to ask, knowing she'd accepted the wedding invitation.

"She'll be here for the weekend," he answered, then Forrest joined them at the door. Bailey slipped away.

She couldn't keep her eyes off Steele, though, when he bent in front of Kevin to show him how to carry the velvet pillow bearing the wedding rings across the yard. "You have to keep it level," he explained. "Pretend the rings are eggs and they'll break if they roll off."

Steele was so big next to the small, sturdy boy, yet so very gentle....

And he belonged to Lana.

"Maybe you should practice with a real egg," Bailey suggested brightly, fighting the ache of loss sweeping through her. Opening the refrigerator, she grabbed one and moved to set it on the pillow at the same time Steele straightened and reached for it. Their hands brushed. Bailey's suddenly nerveless fingers dropped the egg as she snatched back her hand.

Kevin caught the egg on the pillow. Her gaze held by Steele's, Bailey saw him only in her peripheral vision. Steele's eyes seemed to warm, and a grin tugged at his lips.

"Good catch, Kev," he commented, then turned away to follow Forrest and the minister out the back door. When the men reached the canopy, Kevin and Jenny were to walk out together, followed by Bailey.

Her hand tingling from Steele's touch, and her heart rioting in reaction, Bailey felt as if she stood alone, watching and hearing those around her from a great distance.

She heard Bonnie remind the children to walk side by side, as she ushered them out the door. Saw Kevin's forehead pucker with concentration at the task of balancing the egg. And even noticed her parents' proud smiles as they took their places on each side of her sister. Yet still she felt removed, lost in her inner turmoil.

"You're next," Bonnie told her with a wink. Bailey plummeted back to reality. Her sister didn't just mean that it was Bailey's turn to go out the door. She bit her lip to keep from moaning.

She still loved Steele. She'd never love another.

The abbreviated ceremony passed in a blur. She trained her eyes on the minister, willing herself not to look at Steele. She couldn't bear to be near him and know he was forever beyond her reach.

The minute the minister finished, she turned to her mother. "Come help me put the finishing touches on dinner," she said as an excuse to flee. They'd go to a restaurant after the rehearsal on the eve of the wedding but tonight, they were having a barbecue.

"Dad, you start the coals," she called over her shoulder. "Forrest, you mix the drinks." She hurried her mother to the kitchen without waiting for a response.

"What's the rush?" her mother complained when they climbed the steps to the deck.

"Forrest and Steele are big men, they eat a lot." Bailey opened the screen door and ushered her into the kitchen.

"There's not that much to do," her mother still objected. "The potato salad is already made." She sat down at the table. "Come talk to me, you haven't told me much about this Steele. He stares at you when you're not looking."

"I'll just start the baked beans." Bailey pulled a casserole from the refrigerator and shoved it in the oven. The last thing she wanted to do was sit down and discuss Steele. Was he really staring at her, though? "May as well let the steaks warm to room temperature, too." She returned to the refrigerator and pulled out the meat.

"You might want to turn the oven on, the beans will bake much faster that way," her mother said with a fond smile. "What's the matter with you? You're so nervous if I didn't know better, I'd think you were the bride."

The screen door opened. Kevin dashed through the kitchen. "It's okay if I play with the toys from before, isn't it?" he asked without waiting for an answer. Bailey opened her mouth to tell him the toys were no longer there, but Steele filled the doorway, and she lost her voice.

"I told your dad I'd start the fire. Coals in the same place?" He stepped inside and opened the pantry door.

"Bailey!" Kevin raced back into the kitchen. "The toys are gone! Everything's gone!"

"What?" Steele swiveled away from the pantry, his glance darting between Kevin and Bailey. "Show me." Kevin scampered toward the hallway with Steele on his heels.

Bailey leaned against the refrigerator and stared at her mother, unable to hide the effect Steele's presence had on her.

"You know," her mother said with a secretive smile, "while you girls were growing up, I used to dream of a double wedding."

"Sounds like a good idea to me." Steele strode back into the kitchen, not stopping until he towered over Bailey. "Does the change in that room mean you're ready to face the future?"

"I faced the future," Bailey snapped, suddenly finding her voice and straightening her back, "when I sent you back to your family." After the months of loneliness she'd endured, she wasn't going to let him call her a coward, again. Giving him up—and not calling to beg him to come back—had taken every ounce of courage she possessed.

He grinned. "What if I told you Lana doesn't want me any more than I want her?"

Bailey felt her lips move, but her tongue failed to form words. She struggled to absorb his meaning.

"You see, we were kids when we got married," Steele explained. "And we've both grown up. Neither one of us is the same person." He paused to search her face for her reaction.

Bailey blinked once, then twice, to make sure she wasn't dreaming.

Steele rested his hands on the refrigerator, one on each side of her, then lowered his head to nuzzle her cheek. "She lives nearby and sees Kevin regularly, but we're friends, not lovers."

"Not . . . lovers?" Bailey squeaked, holding very still as she felt the warm caress of his lips slide toward hers.

"Definitely—" he brushed his mouth over hers "—not."

She moved her head, lifting her chin to claim the lips tantalizing hers . . . to claim the man she loved.

"Oh, yuck!" Kevin's voice blended with the whirls of happiness spinning inside Bailey's head. "What about the toys?"

"I'm sure Max has a ball you can throw outside," her mother's voice answered. The screen door banged closed behind them. "Bonnie, you were right!" They heard her call. "We're definitely going to need that second rehearsal!"

Steele lifted his head. "A double wedding sound all right to you?"

Too full of emotion to speak, Bailey smiled and nodded through her tears. "What about living in Connecticut?" he asked worriedly. "I live on a lake and have a fenced yard for Max. I'd rather not move Kevin or sell the gym, but I know how close you are to Bonnie. . . ."

Bailey silenced him with a kiss. "Telephones and airplanes will keep us close."

The door opened. A beaming Bonnie and Forrest stepped into the kitchen.

"Skip the telephone, I'll just use my twin antennae," Bonnie said, wagging her fingers over her head.

"You couldn't have known this would happen," Steele protested, "when we didn't!"

Bonnie and Forrest exchanged a smug glance. "You were miserable when I saw you in New York," Forrest began.

"And Bailey was miserable here," Bonnie continued.

"So we put two and two together," Forrest finished, "and gave you time to take care of legalities and join us at the altar."

"I have to have two rehearsals, I'm just so afraid Jenny's going to turn the wedding into a comedy routine," Bailey mimicked her sister, then broke into laughter and hugged first her, then Forrest. Steele followed suit. They went outside to join Bailey and Bonnie's parents and, much to Kevin's disgust, more hugging and kissing followed.

TWO DAYS LATER, Kevin carried four rings on a velvet pillow to the flower-strewn canopy in Bailey's backyard. Proud of her new dress, Jenny pranced beside him, swinging her basket of flowers and crushing the fragile petals with her fist before scattering them on the path.

A tanned, healthier Lana followed the children. On the spur of the moment, Bailey had asked her to be an attendant when she'd met her at the airport with Steele. Lana's gratitude for her rescue and sincere best wishes for their marriage had been so heartfelt, Bailey knew she'd have a friend in Connecticut.

Bailey and Bonnie's mother served as matron of honor, her lined face an older version of the twin brides who were escorted down the aisle by her husband. The sisters wore identical dresses of peach trimmed in ivory and straw hats with wide brims and satin ribbons.

When the three halted before the minister, Steele and Forrest stepped forward to claim their brides without hesitation. The love in Bailey's eyes as she gazed up at him led Steele to her side at the same time Bonnie's drew Forrest.

One by one, they took their vows. Bailey squeezed Steele's hand when the minister intoned, "To love and to cherish," and recited with him:

"From this day forward."